"KEEP YOUR HANDS HIGH..."

The lame man's lips were thick and set at a cruel angle.

"Git off that hoss easy, mister," ordered the man with the rifle.

"I intend doing as you tell me." Slocum raised his hands high above his shoulders.

"Shoot 'im if he blinks," said the man on the crutch.

"I'm getting off," Slocum said. "Don't get nervous with that rifle. I don't want to be shot."

"No sudden moves." The man with the gun smiled crookedly. He looked at the name carved on the saddlebags. "John Slocum, eh? This ain't your lucky day, Johnny boy. Nosiree."

OTHER BOOKS BY JAKE LOGAN

JAKE LOGAN

SLOCUM AND THE BUFFALO HUNTERS

B
BERKLEY BOOKS, NEW YORK

SLOCUM AND THE BUFFALO HUNTERS

A Berkley Book/published by arrangement with
the author

PRINTING HISTORY
Berkley edition/October 1988

ISBN: 0-425-11056-7

10 9 8 7 6 5 4 3 2 1

1

An immense blue sky hung low over the flat green prairie of western Kansas. The gradual swells of the high plains spread out to a seemingly infinite horizon. Now, after a brief thundershower, John Slocum let his horse set the stride along the trail. The animal moved south at a leisurely pace.

The sun had dropped low in the west when the horse smelled water. The animal moved at a trot until a small river came into view. The stream was lined on both banks with weeds, brush, cottonwood, and willow trees. Slocum planned to camp there that night, resting his horse, cooling himself with a long swim.

He was almost to the river when two men jumped out of the bushes. They pointed a battered old flintlock rifle at him and yelled for him to get down and give up his horse and money.

The man holding the gun was thin. He had a pock-

1

marked face. The flintlock gun pointed at Slocum had a split wood stock, and the outside of the iron barrel was corroded.

The second man was fat, lame, and leaned on a crutch fashioned from a cottonwood tree limb. Their clothes were ragged and worn thin. Behind them, something moved in the thicket.

"Git off that hoss easy, mister," ordered the man with the rifle.

"Keep your hands high," snapped the lame man. His lips were thick and set at a cruel angle.

"I intend doing as you tell me." Slocum raised his hands high above his shoulders.

"Shoot 'im if he blinks," said the man on the crutch.

"I'm getting off," Slocum said. "Don't get nervous with that rifle. I don't want to be shot."

"No sudden moves." The man with the gun smiled crookedly. He looked at the name carved on the saddle-bags. "John Slocum, eh? This ain't your lucky day, Johnny boy. No siree."

Slocum swung down out of the saddle.

"I'll git his pistols, Lige," croaked the lame man. "Damnation! He's got two pistols and a rifle. Easy pickin's ag'in!"

The man on the crutch hopped forward as Slocum reached the ground.

The rifleman's attention was distracted by the cripple's faltering movement. He didn't see John Slocum dropped into a crouch, nor did he see the lightning quickness of the fast draw. He felt the lead tear into his stomach, heard the roar of Slocum's exploding pistol, saw the orange flame spurt from the barrel.

Then the robber was driven down by the power of the bullet. As he fell back into the weeds, the man pulled the trigger on the old flintlock rifle. The gun went off with a mighty roar. The ball slammed into the crippled man's spine.

Crying with pain, the crippled man spun around on his makeshift crutch. His hands clawed the air as he spun to the ground. Dazed, with blood spurting from his back, he whimpered like a crazed animal. The big lead ball had blasted a large hole in his back.

Slocum turned his revolver toward the thicket. "Come out with your hands held high!"

"My boys!" The voice was a loud, shrill croak. "You've kilt my young'uns."

"Get out here!"

"I'm a-comin!"

A toothless old hag in a filthy homespun dress stepped out of the thicket. Her rheumy eyes were deeply set in a wrinkled face. Her gray hair was thin and dirty, plastered to the side of her skull.

She looked down at the two wounded men, who moaned and twisted in the dirt.

"Lige, you hurt?" The old woman's voice was thin and reedy.

"Gut shot," groaned the rifleman.

The woman responded. "Ye're good as daid."

"He kilt me, Maw."

The old woman looked down at the wounded cripple. "My baby," she croaked. "My pore chile."

She spun around and glared at Slocum with a feral glitter in her eyes. Her hands shot up, fingers held like the claws of a bird of prey. "You kilt 'em," she cried.

She rushed at Slocum with her dirt-encrusted thumbs thrust out, ready to pop an eyeball from its socket.

John Slocum sidestepped the woman's charge and slammed the barrel of his pistol against the side of her head. She went spinning off into the weeds, squalling like a poleaxed steer.

"Hit wimmin!" she cried. "Ain't fair t'hit wimmin."

Slocum holstered his gun. He walked past the cripple, who sobbed with loud, liquid gasps.

The other man had a raspy sound in his breathing. Slocum bent over and picked the old flintlock rifle out of the weeds. Swinging the rifle high above his head, he tossed the weapon out into the middle of the river. The gun sank out of sight.

Slocum swung up into the saddle.

"Ye can't go," screamed the woman.

"I can and will."

"What about me 'n' my boys?" she cried.

"Ma'am, you and your boys got a hard row to hoe."

The old woman began to scream.

Slocum looked down at the wounded men and shook his head in a negative manner. Without prodding, the horse moved out into the water. Behind him, the three bushwackers cursed and screamed.

Safely across the river, Slocum left the trail and rode along the bank on the south side of the stream. He followed the river until the screams died out. Then he rode another mile beyond that and stopped in a grove of cottonwoods and willows.

He never glanced back to the crossing at the river. That incident was behind him, and, while he didn't enjoy violence, he would kill to survive. The old woman and her sons had probably killed many travelers. The frontier was better off without them.

After a pleasant swim, he caught three sunfish and grilled them over a small fire. He picked a handful of wild berries for his dessert. Then he rode until sunset and made dry camp on the prairie. He figured two days' of riding would bring him to Dodge City.

John Slocum was starting to feel like a new man. The trail dust, dirt, and grime were soaking off his body into the soapy water at the Dodge City Bath House. Slocum had showered first, then spent two hours in an iron bathtub filled with hot soapy water. The bath was a nice beginning for his visit to Dodge City, Kansas.

Periodically, the old Chinaman who owned the establishment added another bucket of steaming hot water to the bath. The smiling Oriental padded into the room on straw sandals, carrying the pail of water that had been heated on a large iron stove in the rear of the clapboard and tarpaper building.

The man was dressed in black coolie clothes. He had established the bath house when Dodge City became the Kansas end of the cattle trail from Texas. Horsemen who came to Dodge City from any direction arrived with a thick layer of trail dust on their bodies and clothes. Men like Slocum made the bath house their first stop in the cow town.

"Is your business doing good?" Slocum asked.

"Business fine," smiled the old man. "No time to eat lunch. Me go eat now. Go home and take nap."

"You want me to get out?" Slocum asked.

"No! No!" The man clasped his hands together, bowed low. "Honorable customer enjoy bath. May Ling wash and iron your clothes. She in back. You need anything, yell for May Ling."

The smiling Chinaman bowed low and backed out of the room. He disappeared behind a pair of beaded curtains. Slocum laid his head on the folded towel on the back of the tub. He closed his eyes and relaxed.

The ride out of Nebraska had been grueling. Slocum had been in North Platte when a sharp-eyed sheriff found an old "Wanted—Dead or Alive" poster in a bottom drawer of his desk. There was enough information on the wanted poster to arouse the lawman's suspicion.

A newcomer from the East who had failed as a homesteader, the sheriff figured Slocum's arrest would be good for headlines. Good news coverage would convince the voters of the sheriff's ability as a lawman. A friendly deputy knew the wanted poster was old, probably in error, and nothing but trouble for North Platte and John Slocum. He passed a warning to the man from Calhoun County, Georgia, who packed up and headed out of town. With no particular destination in mind, Slocum flipped a coin to decide what direction to travel in.

The ride south out of North Platte had been rugged because the country was boiling in a heat wave. Grasshoppers, locusts, and vermin of every type plagued Slocum and his horse. The attempted robbery at the river crossing didn't surprise him. A man was ready for bushwackers when he rode alone on the plains.

When Slocum arrived in Dodge City, his first stop was at the livery stable. He ordered extra oats and corn for his horse and tipped the groom to curry the animal. When his horse was unsaddled and watered, Slocum headed for the bath house.

Now, Slocum's reveries were ended by a delicate cough coming from the rear of the bath house. He glanced up as the curtains parted and a petite Chinese girl came into the room. She wore a floor-length green silk robe with Oriental symbols embroidered on it.

The young woman averted her eyes as she approached Slocum's tub. "Papa go to lunch," she said. "May Ling is boss. Closed sign put on door. You need more hot water?"

"Naw, I'm about done," Slocum said. "Another ten minutes and I'll turn into a prune."

She smiled. "May Ling think you dirty man."

"You're May Ling?" Slocum was pleased with her sparkling black eyes, her golden skin. "Maybe you could wash my back."

"At honorable customer's service." The girl bowed low with a mocking smile. "What customer want, he get. Honorable father teach May Ling to please."

Slocum grinned. "Is that a fact?"

"Is true."

"Your father is a very wise man."

"May Ling think so." She picked up a long-handled brush from a shelf above the tub and began to brush Slocum's back with a vigorous motion.

Slocum sighed. "You have a nice touch."

"You have nice body. May Ling like hard bodies."

"Shucks, I'll bet you say that to all of your customers."

"Not true," the Chinese girl protested. "May Ling peek when you take off clothes. You have nice body."

Slocum laughed. "Thank you very much."

"Is true," May Ling giggled. She laid down the brush and picked up a cake of soap. "Here, I lather good."

John Slocum stretched out in the iron bathtub. May Ling's hand dipped beneath the foamy surface of the bathwater. Her palm glided down across Slocum's hard stomach. Her delicate fingers circled his growing hardness. Her hand made a stroking motion in the water as her lips kissed Slocum's chin.

"Real big one," husked May Ling. "You want to do it?"

"You're reading my mind."

May Ling's hand came up out of the water. She pulled a large towel off a rack. "Get dry. We go in back room. May Ling show you an Oriental mystery."

Slocum stood up in the tub, water pouring off his body. He reached for the towel, but May Ling shook her head negatively. She came forward and rubbed a warm towel over his skin, first gently, then with a strong pressure.

"Umm, that feels good," Slocum said.

"Follow May Ling."

The young Chinese woman took Slocum's hand and led him through the beaded curtains into the back room. This area of the building contained a large iron stove, several washtubs, and an ironing board. His clothes had been washed, ironed, and hung over a wooden clothes rack.

"We go to parlor," May Ling said. She took Slocum's hand and led him through another pair of thick curtains. "This is May Ling's favorite room."

Slocum felt as if he was entering a splendid Oriental temple dedicated to love. A single padded mattress covered with dark red silk occupied one corner. The pad was partially surrounded by two black straw screens woven like a priceless tapestry. A black-laquered chest and a small chair were the only furniture in the room.

"You like?" May Ling asked.

"Beautiful."

"May Ling want you be happy. Lay down."

Following her directions, Slocum eased his nude body down on the mattress.

May Ling giggled. "Too tall," she whispered, pointing at Slocum's feet sticking out over the end of the mattress. "You like feel?"

Slocum wiggled on the silk coverlet. "Very smooth."

"How 'bout this feel?" May Ling knelt beside him, and her fingers grasped his swelling erection. She watched the flesh harden, lengthen.

"You're a wonderment," Slocum said.

"Ummm." May Ling's head dipped low and her lips were open wide. Then her warm mouth slowly engulfed his pulsating flesh. Her tongue made a series of tiny, pulsating movements, calculated and deliberate, like a butterfly's wings fluttering in the wind.

Next, the intensity of her mouth increased and Slocum's body arced up to meet her. Then, with a pleasurable release, he was freed from the tension. He looked down and the only thing he could see was May Ling's mass of dark black hair.

Then the Chinese girl turned around and grinned. "Welcome to Dodge City," she said. "What's your name?"

"Lucky man," Slocum answered. "Better known as John Slocum."

After paying his bill and giving a big tip to May Ling, John Slocum checked into the Dodge House. The opulent hotel was touted as being the most luxurious west of Chicago. The cow town was swarming with visitors, and sleeping rooms were scarce. However, a five-dollar tip improved the desk clerk's memory—miraculously, the bespectacled man remembered a room that had just been vacated by a salesman.

After checking in, Slocum went for a walk down by the railroad tracks. The corrals along the Santa Fe line were crammed with cattle awaiting shipment to the packing-houses in Chicago. He was told that dozens of other herds were being held south of town until corral space opened up.

Throngs of men crowded the streets of Dodge City. They drifted from the Long Branch Saloon, over to the Alamo, the Lady Gay, the Naughty Lady, or the Cattle-man's Delight. Or, they wandered into the Delmonico Restaurant to wolf down oysters, crabmeat, and other unusual foods.

After the long trip north out of Texas to the railhead, the cattlemen paid off their cowhands in cash. With several months' pay in their pockets, the Texans were ready to party. They were a loud, boisterous bunch of men looking for a good time and plenty of excitement.

Feeling thirsty, John Slocum entered the Naughty Lady Saloon on Front Street. Beyond the batwing doors was a large hall filled with cowboys, buffalo hunters, hiders, Indian scouts, soldiers from Fort Dodge, and railroad men. A couple of plaid-suited salesmen leaned against the bar, watching the crowd swill down the booze.

Slocum eased his way through the drinkers and found a small table at the back of the saloon. He sat down and ordered a beer from a waiter, who wore a long white apron.

John Slocum was starting to feel at home in Dodge City. After the long ride out of Nebraska, he figured the good life consisted of wine, women, and song. He had discov-ered the women were wild in Dodge City, the wine was undoubtedly aged and expensive, and bawdy songs could be heard in every saloon in town.

The evening's entertainment at the Naughty Lady was provided by a trio of musicians. The tall, lanky fiddler had a down-home Southern style of playing. His music reminded Slocum of the barn dances he'd attended back in Calhoun County, Georgia, before the Civil War.

The fiddler was accompanied by a talented, fat piano player with a derby hat perched on his bald head. The piano player was known in Dodge City as Skulltop. The third musician was the drummer, who embellished the songs with a sharp, crisp stroke across the drumhead.

Although the musicians were talented, the true appeal of the Naughty Lady was the hostesses. This was the saloon's term for twenty women who danced with the customers. The women wore frilly red dresses with low-cut bodices that revealed a generous flash of flesh. Their faces were caked with powder and paint.

The rough, gritty Texans in the Naughty Lady were ready to dance until the last woman was swept off her feet. They didn't care if the women were a little past their prime. They had been smelling the hind side of a herd of longhorn steers since leaving Texas. They were happy because the hostesses were feminine, sweet-smelling, and able to shake a leg and other body parts on the dance floor.

Now the music stopped and the dancers drifted back to their tables or over to the bar. Slocum smiled as one of the saloon girls walked back to his table and sat down. She wore a red satin dress that hugged her curves. Her brown hair was cut short, and on the side of it she wore a tiny gold hat. She said her name was Maureen Polk and wasn't Dodge City really booming.

"Now, John Slocum," she said, brightly. "Tell me what you're doing in Dodge City."

John Slocum looked blank.

2

Maureen Polk was twenty-seven years old, the widow of a riverboat gambler from St. Louis. Her husband's major error in a short and degenerate life was letting two kings fall out of his ruffled sleeve during a big-money poker game on a steamboat. Another player, a businessman from Keokuk, Iowa, pulled a derringer, shot at point-blank range, and killed the gambler.

When her husband was buried, Maureen totaled up her assets. She had thirteen dollars, a ticket to Kansas City on the side-wheeler, and a sure knowledge of what men liked. Always an optimistic girl with a yen for adventure, Maureen looked upon widowhood as an opportunity. Besides, she was tired of watching men smoke, drink, and play cards. She wanted attention and interesting men to court for her favors.

Maureen had smooth skin beneath a thick layer of powder and rouge. The first slackness of a double chin was evident, and her hips were thickening. Her large bright brown eyes twinkled with humor as she sat across the table from Slocum.

"John Slocum," she said. "It sure is good to see you."

"How are you?" Slocum wondered who she was.

"The night has barely started and I'm wor out." Maureen eased her feet out of her high-heeled patent leather shoes. She rubbed her feet together. "We met someplace. Maybe Newton, Abilene, or Ellsworth. Your name is John Slocum. I remember you were a great poker player and you made a good impression on me as a virile lover."

John smiled. "Want a drink?"

"Naw, they'd bring some colored water. Let the Texans pay for that."

"How long have you been in Dodge City?"

"Too long. I need a place to curl up quietly and die."

"You're too young for that." Slocum had a dim memory of the woman. They had spent a night in a room over a saloon, three or four years ago. He could not recall the name of the town where they had met.

Maureen Polk was just one of the ladies he had bedded down since coming west. Actresses, dance hall girls, lady preachers, Indian maidens, and whores—enough women to fill a valley. Some were a physical diversion for a single night, while others were entertainment for a week, a month, or longer.

Some of the women had been soft and feminine; others were as hard as the country they lived in. They came in every size, weight, and degree of sexual preference. Now, his desire sated by the Chinese girl, Slocum looked upon Maureen as an old friend.

"I never realized a life of sin required so much energy," Maureen said. "I used to think whoring would be an easy way to make a living. All a gal had to do was lay back and let the men do the grunting, groaning, and heavy lifting."

"You should find a good man and settle down," Slocum advised.

"I never cared for raising kids, or being a servant to some hod carrier. Even as a little slip of a girl I wanted to be a whore. It looked like the ideal life for a lazy lady like me."

Slocum grinned, making a sweeping gesture with his hands. "Well, your dream came true."

"I thought a gal could sit all day eating candy and petting her poodle dog," Maureen said. "By now, I should be fighting off handsome men with my powder puff. I always thought men were supposed to give presents or money to their favorite fancy woman, sweet little Maureen. In my foolish girlhood, I thought putting out was enough to keep a few men on the hook. Naturally, housecleaning and the dirty dishes would be done by the ugly girls."

Slocum laughed. "Even ugly girls need a man."

Maureen blinked her brown eyes. "They can have these cattlemen. This profession may be one of the oldest, but it is being gnawed to death by horny Texas cowboys. You'd think Texas didn't have women. These jaspers act like animals."

"They've been on the trail for months."

"What these yahoos need is lots of schooling for manners," Maureen went on. "They're too rambunctious. Last night I was abused by a sorry-looking little sonofabitch. A regular runt filled with whiskey and dirty thoughts. He grabbed my breast when I was doing the Virginia reel with another fellow. Honest, this skinny warthog almost tore my tit off. He hung on like a leech, swinging from my breast, if you know what I mean."

"I get the picture," Slocum said. He leaned over and gave a suggestive glance at the top of Maureen's breasts displayed by the low-cut gown.

"Get your eyeballs off there!" Maureen's voice was laced with mock anger. "I never fiddle-faddle with old friends."

"Spoken like a lady with a heart of gold," Slocum replied. "Now, you were telling me about this runt swinging from your amply endowed body appendage. What happened?"

"It was painful. I thought he was gonna tear it off. Finally, the bouncer grabbed him by the neck and threw him out in the street. The little rat landed beside the horse trough and laid there, kicking and yelling that he'd copped a feel."

Slocum laughed. "You have a weird effect on men, Maureen."

"It ain't my fault, honey. Besides, I know what they're after."

"Companionship."

"Call it what you want." Maureen looked at Slocum with a heavy-lidded expression. "I never heard it called that."

"Nature's natural remedy?"

She smiled. "Honey, I just shake it, sit on it, and sell it."

"An honest woman."

"You won't ever see me pussyfooting around the bush," she giggled.

"But you will for a couple of dollars?" John Slocum raised an eyebrow.

"Money gets my juices flowing, Slocum. Why else would I be in Dodge City?" She picked up her shoes and started pushing the shiny pumps on her feet. "Present company doesn't count. I'll tell you a little secret, baby. Most of these cowboys smell like the dogs fought over them for a week in somebody's backyard."

"Cattle trails don't have bath houses."

"Maybe so, but they could clean up here in Dodge before hitting the saloons," Maureen said. "You're nice and clean. Your clothes look good. You've probably been over to the bath house and messing with that Chinese girl. I don't like amateur competition, but at least May Ling turns them out clean and nice-smelling. I'm for everyone having a slanty-eyed lady on the side if she runs a bath house and does laundry and ironing."

"I guess," Slocum said.

"Don't sit there looking like the Sante Fe locomotive just ran over your private parts," said Maureen. "You figured that Chinese girl did it because she liked you? Like everyone else, you probably left her a big tip. Hell, Slocum, one dumb woman can outsmart an army of men. She just tells every man that he's the only one, that he overwhelmed her. Now, how long have you been in Dodge?"

"I just got in."

"Staying awhile."

"The town looks exciting."

"And expensive, honey," said Maureen. "I hope you have a poke full of cash. That's the only medium of exchange in this cow town."

"I'm not starving," Slocum answered.

"Payday doesn't last long here."

"I didn't come up with a herd."

"What are you doing?"

"Just looking. I may do a little gambling."

Maureen smiled. "The Texans are ripe for picking."

"Then I'm a farmer ready to harvest," Slocum grinned.

The sound of a bow being drawn over violin strings came from the front of the saloon. The piano player adjusted his hat and bent over the keyboard. The drummer sat down, hit a few licks, and the music started. Several customers left the bar and headed for the dance floor looking for a partner.

"Time to earn a living," Maureen stood up.

"Happy dancing," Slocum said. He twisted around in his chair to watch the woman's departure.

A half-dozen men headed toward the saloon girl. She darted away from a beefy, burly man with a long, untrimmed beard. Next she eluded a greasy-looking buffalo hunter, sidestepped a trapper, and looked around for someone with clean clothes.

Suddenly a salesman ran out on the floor. Maureen was swept up into the embrace of the tall, plaid-suited man. He grinned and grabbed her arms, dancing with surprising ease in tune with the music.

Slocum started to ease his chair back against the wall.

He felt hard metal in the middle of his back.

"Hold it," a man's voice said. "Hands on the table, cowboy. You're John Slocum or I'm a stinkweed among flowers."

Slocum didn't move.

"Now, you addle-headed drifter, say hello to your old friend, Bat Masterson." The voice took on a friendly lilt.

Slocum turned around and looked into the smiling face of William Barclay Masterson, who had entered the saloon through the back door. Masterson held a small metal cigar case in his hand.

Masterson was a slender young man dressed in a black suit, red cravet, and ruffled shirt. A black bowler hat was perched on top of his head. His black hair was neatly trimmed. A tarnished tin star was pinned to the right lapel of his suit.

Slocum snorted. "I see you still like funny hats."

"You don't know fashion." Masterson removed his hat and twirled the bowler on his index finger. "The latest fashion. Beats that flat-topped sombrero of yours, Slocum. You're too backwoodsy. The boys from the country don't know gentlemanly attire. Lord, you'd be amazed at the looks I get from the Texans. They're not certain if I'm a sissy boy or a deluxe pistolero."

"Sit down." Slocum gestured toward a chair. "It's darn good to see you, but your greeting made my heart stop."

"Never let your guard down."

"I got interested in what the lady was saying," Slocum said.

"Which one?"

"Maureen."

Masterson signaled the waiter for a round of drinks.

"She's a beaut. Getting long in the tooth, however. Another couple years of this life and she'll be working the cribs. That's how it goes when you're peddling flesh."

Slocum asked, "When did you start wearing the tin star?"

"A couple months ago."

"Deputy sheriff?"

"I'm the assistant town marshal."

"Who told you I was in town?"

"You rascal! You've been studying mysteries." Masterson laughed. "Any truth to those rumors about Asian ladies?"

"What rumors?" Slocum pretended to be puzzled.

"You never heard about Chinese women?"

"Nope."

"For one thing they have a big mouth."

Slocum smiled. "She knows how to use it."

"You meet her father?" Masterson asked.

"A nice old guy," Slocum said. "Does he know about May Ling's specialty?"

"That's another mystery. No one knows for sure. I expect they're working together. But I'm not sure. Maybe someday he'll come back too quick. Then I'll find someone with a Chinese hatchet in their head. So watch yourself, good buddy."

"I will," Slocum promised. "You saved my life, and I'm not going to throw it away. Remember the good times down in Texas?"

The waiter brought over a whiskey and water for Masterson, another beer for Slocum. Then the two men toasted their friendship and recalled when they met in Texas.

Several Panhandle ranchers were battling over land and water rights during a screw-your-neighbor fracas after the Civil War. Each side in the dispute began to hire gunhands. Slocum hired out for one faction; Masterson rode for the opposing side.

After a few skirmishes, the gunmen decided someone

could get killed over what was a senseless argument. An agreement was made between both groups of gunfighters. They would blast away, fast and furious, to please the ranchers paying their wages. But everyone would aim high or to the side. The ranchers would be impressed, and the gunhands would live to spend their money.

After the pact was made, the countryside echoed with gunfire. Men chased each other across the range, shooting, yelling, running back to the bunkhouse for more ammunition. Altogether, it was a satisfactory way to spend a summer and earn a few dollars.

Then, a hardcase named Wes Lassiter hired onto Masterson's side of the dispute. He was a loner, a man with a nasty temper and blood lust. Lassiter bragged about the notches on his gun butt and claimed to be the meanest man in either camp.

Lassiter swore a true gunfighter would never defraud an employer. He planned to bushwhack Slocum, shooting from ambush from across the street from the local saloon. Learning of the plan, Masterson and a few friends overpowered Lassiter.

They took away his guns and threw him on a stagecoach leaving town. The shotgun guard agreed to take the blood-thirsty gunman to the end of the line. The great range war continued until the feuding ranchers agreed to a truce.

Now, Masterson ordered more drinks.

"I'll get this round," Slocum said.

"Save your money. The house runs a free tab for the marshals and his friends."

"Free booze. That's a good benefit."

"Peacemaking has some good moments," said Masterson. "Not many. Once in a while you see a hint of daylight."

"The gunmen here don't aim high and wide?"

"We're not conning the city fathers. But Wyatt and me love sucking the public tit. It beats heavy lifting."

"Dangerous?"

"Not much."

"I hear different."

Masterson shook his head negatively. "It isn't bad. The amateurs are easy to handle. We don't have that many professionals coming to town on the prod. Either me or Wyatt Earp—he's also marshaling—know most of them. An occasional gent comes through wanting to make a name for himself. They think long and hard after hearing we're not into giving away our lives. If we can't talk sense to them, we've found that a sawed-off Greener shotgun in the belly gets the point across real fast. Now, what have you been up to?"

Slocum asked, "You know anything about an old lady and a couple of boys north of here?"

"Old lady Bender and her boys."

"Killers?"

"Rattlers of the worst kind," answered Masterson. "They rob, waylay, and bushwhack. The old woman is vicious. She'll kill for the fun of it. The boys have a thirst for blood."

"Why hasn't someone done them in?"

Masterson shrugged. "They bushwhack a nester or a couple of riders, bury the bodies, and who's to know? They were run out of Ford County about a year ago. The local folks just got fed up with their way of life. They didn't do anything you could arrest them for. But you knew they were darn guilty of something."

"Where did they go?"

"They've been up north living in a sod house near a river. The oldest boy is named Lige, a snake. He never did a single act of kindness for anyone. Marty is crippled. They're all blood crazy."

"They won't be bothering anyone in the future."

"They try something with you?"

Slocum explained the events at the river crossing. When he was finished, Masterson shook his hand and congratulated the man from Georgia for exterminating vermin in the state of Kansas.

"Fact is," said Masterson, "your efforts deserve some real recognition. You're invited to a poker game tonight. Wyatt Earp, me, and you will sit in against a cattleman. High stakes. Wyatt and I have been doing fairly well. Texans don't know the odds. They're always anxious to show their expertise with the pasteboards."

"What time and where at?" Slocum had a bankroll of slightly more than four hundred dollars. He would enjoy the opportunity to run his wad up to maybe five hundred.

"Nine o'clock," said Masterson. "The back room of the Long Branch Saloon."

"I'll be there."

Masterson stood up. "The cattleman's name is Texas Tom Schacht. Know him?"

"Nope."

"Says he sold about eleven hundred head of cattle. He should be loaded. I have to make my rounds of the saloons. See you at nine?"

"I'll be there," Slocum promised.

3

The band at the Naughty Lady Saloon laid down their instruments and took a break. Maureen Polk fended off the amorous advances of the plaid-suited salesman, slipped out of the saloon, and hurried down the street to a small clapboard house set back on a weed-covered lot.

The front room of the house contained an old horsehair sofa, a couple of oak chairs, and a square wooden table. Texas Tom Schacht, the gambler's alias, was playing solitaire.

"I met a good prospect," Maureen said.

Texas Tom looked up from the cards. "No cowboys. I'm tired of trail hands. They raise cain over losing fifty bucks.."

"This guy is loaded," Maureen lied.

Texas Tom Schacht smiled. "Maybe you're worth the effort, Maureen. Tell me about him."

Texas Tom Schacht had been a partner at one time with

Maureen Polk's dead husband. Schacht was a tall man dressed in a pair of cattleman's jeans, a cotton shirt, a string tie, and a pair of medium-heeled stockman's boots.

A gunbelt with a Remington bone-handled pistol was lying on the table. Schacht wore the gun because it was part of the role he was playing. He also carried a small hideout derringer in the top of his boot.

Texas Tom Schacht had been born in upstate New York, the son of a farmer and former stage magician and his wife. His real name was Enos Pruett. Early on he was tutored by his father in sleight of hand. Relatives and friends expected the clever boy to be a headliner in show business.

On his eleventh birthday the boy was the guest at a party on his uncle's farm. While the other children played outdoors, little Enos stayed inside and watched the men play cards. He was awed by the money. He observed that playing cards offered easy money—provided you always won.

Within a year the boy was an accomplished card mechanic. He could shuffle an unmarked deck, deal the cards, and know which player held the high cards. He continued to practice until his parents complained about the chores not being done. After a few whippings from his father, the lad ran away from home. He wandered through New England playing poker, seeing the sights, and obtaining an education as a gambler.

Soon he grew tired of travel and took a room above a tavern outside of Lawrence, Massachusetts. He played poker and made love to the girls who worked in the city's textile mills. The games around Lawrence did not involve big money, so Enos won only enough to pay his expenses.

During a high-stakes game one night, Enos was unable to resist taking several pots. One of the losers complained to the police. The next morning a policeman arrested Enos, confiscated his winnings, and tossed the young man in jail. He was sentenced to the local workhouse on a charge of not having any visible means of support.

After his release, he left Lawrence. Traveling west, he built up a bankroll and started to gamble again. He changed his name as he moved from town to town. His winnings were spent on high living, expensive liquor, and pretty women.

He worked the riverboats until his face became too well known. Then he moved from town to town, never hitting too hard on the local players, never busting a man completely. He knew people became angry when a stranger walked away with their last cent.

Now, calling himself Texas Tom Schacht, the gambler listened to Maureen Polk chatter about the hardships of whoring. She was a bother at times, but her instincts about men were good. She could spot a stranger with money before he got off his horse. Good whores had that ability, almost smelling the amount of money in a man's pockets.

Whistling to himself, and not minding Maureen's chatter, Texas Tom Schacht quit his game of solitaire. He dressed for the game at the Long Branch Saloon, looking forward to the action.

Bat Masterson was sitting behind the green-felt-topped table when John Slocum walked into the back room of the Long Branch Saloon.

"Looks like the others are late," said Masterson. "I hope Wyatt gets here. He had to go break up a fight down by the tracks. Take your pick of the chairs."

Slocum sat down in a chair backed against the wall. "Anything serious?"

"Two cowpokes fighting over who's best."

"At what?"

Masterson shrugged. "Who knows? Probably anything you want to mention."

A tall man in cattleman's clothing walked into the room. "I'm Tom Schacht," he said. "This where the game is?"

Masterson made introductions. "Wyatt's running late," he said.

Schacht sat down. "I don't get much action down home," he drawled.

"You may not find it here," said Slocum.

"Well, maybe some fresh people in the game will change my luck," said Schacht. "I haven't been winning much lately."

"I know the feeling." Masterson didn't look sympathetic. "Maybe I can round up a couple players to sit in."

"Good idea," Schacht said. "No professionals. I don't like playing with them."

Masterson left the room and went out into the barroom area.

Schacht and Slocum chatted about the weather, the price of cattle, and the settlement of the west.

"You sell your herd in Dodge?" Slocum asked.

"Naw," Schacht lied. "I went north and sold to the army. They're always needing beef."

Masterson came back with three men in tow. He made introductions but no one remembered the names.

"Let's play poker," Masterson said, sitting down and opening a new deck of cards.

"Okay by me," said a newcomer, a businessman.

"Deal," said a man in an Army uniform with sergeant's stripes.

"What's the limit?" The third man was the plaid-suited salesman who had danced earlier with Maureen Polk. "Unlucky at love. Maybe I'll be a winner at cards."

"Where you from?" asked the sergeant.

"Kansas City," replied the salesman. "McGilligan Brothers Wholesale Hardware."

"Calls on me a couple times a year," said the businessman. "I'm Ed Pearson. Pearson Hardware and ranch supplies."

"Are we gonna play or gab?" asked Slocum.

"All right." Masterson started dealing the cards. "Here, Schacht, cut them."

The cut was made and Masterson started dealing. "Five card stud," he announced.

The players pulled silver from their pockets, and piled the coins in stacks before them.

During the next hour, no one really won. The money moved to and fro across the green felt table. Then, the pace of the cards changed and Slocum won several pots. The main loser in the game was Texas Tom Schacht, who seemed to bet on hands that couldn't stand up.

Soon, the silver stacked up in front of Slocum and the paper money began to appear. Masterson was losing consistently, starting to grouse and complain. The other winner was the salesman in the plaid suit. The rest of the players were down.

Ed Pearson, the hardware storeowner, became talkative. The businessman's strategy in a poker game was to distract his opponents with conversation.

"Passing through?" he asked Slocum.

"Probably."

"Stop by the store before you leave town. I got some deals on saddles."

The salesman chimed in. "He's not blowing smoke. Right, Ed?"

"I got to clear inventory," Pearson said. "Season will be coming to an end. I don't want to carry everything over till next year."

"Quit doing business," snapped Masterson, who was dealing. "You got a queen, Ed. You want to bet?"

"Yeah. A dollar."

Everyone called the bet.

"I raise two dollars," said Schacht.

Everyone met the raise. Masterson passed out the third of the five cards to come.

"Going anywhere in particular?" asked Pearson.

"Nowhere in mind." Slocum had a jack and a five of clubs lying on the table.

"Good opportunity in Texas," drawled Schacht.

"Might look it over."

"We need good men down home."

"Where is that?" asked the salesman.

"Delhart is the closest town."

"Never heard of it," said Ed.

"Nice area."

"I got a feeling of looking for someplace else to start my business," said Ed. "Dodge City is bound to play out someday. The Texas Panhandle sounds good to me."

"That's a lousy location. Speaking of play," snapped the Army sergeant, "saddle sales or not, you're still high. You bettin' or folding?"

"Bet the ace or shut up, Ed," snapped Masterson.

"A buck."

"Bump it up two more," said Schacht. He figured the time had come to get some real money on the table. "Naw, make it five bucks. I'm tired of playing for coins. I'm going home a winner or busted."

"Five bucks?" the sergeant's eyebrows went up. "Bat said this was a friendly game."

"It is," Masterson answered.

"Anyone object?" asked Schacht.

"I got no complaints." Slocum shoved his money into the pot.

Everyone else went along.

"What's wrong with the Panhandle?" Ed wanted to know.

"What's wrong?" echoed the sergeant. "How about Kiowas, Cheyenne, and Comanches. Dull Knife and his band have been on the warpath for a month. Or haven't you heard about their raids?"

"I keep up on everything," answered Ed.

"Try keeping up with the game," said the sergeant.

The flow of betting continued, and the pot, around sixty dollars, went to Ed Pearson, the hardware storekeeper. He grinned like an Indian with a full barrel of firewater.

"I like winning," Pearson said, stacking the coins and

bills neatly in front of his place at the table. "Thank you for the cards, Bat. I love playing poker."

"Bad winners are worse than bad losers," growled the sergeant.

The deal went to Texas Tom Schacht, who decided the moment had arrived to make money from the assembled players. Schacht scooped up the cards, shuffled, and slid them across the table. Slocum cut.

As Schacht was pulling back the deck, his hand shot out and slapped against Ed Pearson's shoulder. "Mosquito," Schacht roared.

Everyone directed their attention to Pearson's chair.

Ed Pearson winced and ducked his head. "Lord! Don't make a riot out of it. Don't you folks have mosquitos in Texas?"

"Not the size of turkey buzzards," said Schacht. "Did I get him?"

"Who cares? Play cards." This came from the salesman from Kansas City.

"Yeah, deal," said Masterson.

"Just wanted to keep the man from a bad bite."

The mosquito gambit always worked. The distraction of the player's attention gave Texas Tom Schacht the time he needed to switch decks. The regular deck of cards had been slipped into his pocket. A rigged deck was now in his hands, ready for the deal.

"Dealer's choice," Schacht drawled. "Schacht is my name. Five-card draw is the game."

Fumbling as if he was a man with ten thumbs, Schacht passed out the cards. The deck had been rigged so that every player received a hand that required strong betting, seemingly a sure-fire winner.

Slocum received four kings with a seven of spades kicker.

Masterson held three eights and two fives.

The hardware merchant had received two nines, two tens, and the jack of diamonds.

The sergeant was breathing heavy, staring at what was possibly a small straight.

The salesman held three jacks, a five, and an eight.

Schacht laid down the deck. One of the more enjoyable moments in a rigged hand was watching the other players try to act normal.

Bat Masterson stroked the edge of the table with a short, spastic movement.

John Slocum looked at his cards with an expressionless face.

He's a cool one, thought Schacht.

The other players twisted, scratched their chins, looked up at the ceiling. Pearson had stopped talking as little beads of sweat appeared on his forehead.

Betting started out at a furious pace. Real money started hitting the green felt. Soon, fifty- and hundred-dollar bets were made. It came time to discard whatever cards the player wanted to replace.

Pearson began to chatter again. "What about those Indians?" he asked the sergeant.

"Later," said the sergeant. "I wanna remember what everyone gets for cards."

"Hell," laughed Masterson. "There can't be more'n five or six hundred dollars on the table. Why get excited?"

When the discards were made, the betting resumed in a fast manner. Now men began to dig into their wallets, purses, and pockets for their bankrolls.

Slocum was worried. The four kings were worth betting every cent he had, but he didn't want to run short. He'd seen men stay with a pot, the bets go sky-high, and end up unable to make the last bet.

Across the table, Texas Tom Schacht gauged every player's strength in money. He was orchestrating the play in a subtle, easy fashion.

The salesman from Kansas City was the first to break. "I'm running thin. Are markers any good?"

"How much?" asked Masterson.

"A hundred."

"Try the local bank," said the sergeant.

"I'm dropping out." The salesman folded, cursing.

First one, then another of the players dropped out as the betting between Schacht and Slocum continued.

"Too rich for me," commented Masterson, throwing his cards face down on the table.

Another round and Ed Pearson wiped his forehead and dropped out.

Next came the sergeant, who looked longingly at his month's pay lying in the pot.

"Leaves you and me," Schacht told Slocum.

"Raise fifty," Slocum replied.

Schacht shoved fifty dollars in the pot. "I call. What have you got?"

Slocum smiled. "Four kings." The man from Georgia started to reach for the pot.

"Wait a minute!" A slight smile tugged at the edge of Schacht's mouth. He laid down his hand. "Four aces beats four kings in Texas."

Slocum's face went slack. "You win it."

"Never heard of such a hand," swore Ed Pearson. "Thank God I got out."

"No wonder you was bumping things up," sighed the salesman, staring at the aces.

"Primed for bear," said Masterson.

"Thank you, gentleman." Schacht raked in the pot. He stuffed the money into his pocket. Then he slid the deck to Ed Pearson. "Your deal, Ed."

"I'm tired of cards." Pearson had lost almost two hundred dollars in the game. "My wife is gonna kill me."

"You better give me a big order, Ed, or I'm in trouble," said the salesman.

The sergeant sighed. "Whatever I do, my paycheck never lasts more than a night in Dodge."

"We breaking up?" asked Masterson.

"I'm buying drinks," said Schacht. "Did I break you, Slocum?"

"Damned near."

Schacht reached in his pocket and pulled out a twenty-dollar bill.

"Consider it a loan," he said, handing the bill to Slocum. "I've been hard up. Pay me when we meet down the road."

Slocum picked up the bill. "Appreciate it."

"I can use a good hand on my ranch," said Schacht.

Masterson tried to smile, although his face was grim. "This is how you get your ranch hands, eh? Bust them in poker and make them work it out."

Schacht stood up. "Gents, I'm buying a few rounds. Let's adjourn to the bar."

"I go home drunk and Emma will kill me," said Pearson, shaking his head.

"She'll kill you when she hears what you lost," replied the salesman. "Either way, you're in trouble."

"Then I might as well get plastered on Schacht's money."

"A noble idea," Masterson agreed.

The group went into the barroom of the Long Branch and sat at a table at the side of the saloon. After drinks were ordered and paid for, Texas Tom Schacht excused himself and went through the back door. He went to the outhouse behind the saloon and pulled the hidden deck of cards from his pocket. He dropped them into the hole.

Then, smiling cheerfully, he returned to the Long Branch and enjoyed the company of the other players.

4

John Slocum knew his poker losses would mean leaving Dodge City. His slender resources meant every penny would have to be spent carefully. The morning after the card game, Slocum checked out of the Dodge House. Then he walked over to the livery stable and paid his bill. He was saddling up when Bat Masterson came strolling down the street.

"You leaving town?" Masterson asked.

"I can't afford to hang around. Prices are too high," Slocum admitted. "I got about five dollars left."

Masterson smiled. "I know where a man can make good money—fast."

Slocum laughed. "No more poker games for me."

"Do you know about Buffalo Center?"

"Nope, that must be a new town."

"Not much of a place," Masterson went on. "Set up to cash in on the buffalo-hide boom. Hunters and hiders make

31

good money, and they spend it. Anyway, I know a man out there who's looking for a good marksman. You could save a wad in a hurry."

Masterson explained that the man, Shawnee Mike Samuelson, was looking for a crack shot. "He offered me a dollar for every buffalo I downed," the marshal explained. "He supplies the gun and ammunition. All you do is blow them away."

"That could be real money," Slocum agreed.

"Samuelson wants to start up another crew. You'd also have to boss a few skinners and hiders. They're a rough bunch, but I figure you can handle them."

"What are hides bringing now?"

"Four and a quarter here in Dodge."

"That's high."

"Buffalo are starting to get scarce," said Masterson.

"Who is Samuelson?"

"An old mountain man."

"Never heard of him."

"He kept a low profile. Went up the Missouri as a kid, trapping beaver for the American Fur Company."

Slocum looked skeptical. "Old mountain men can be hard as granite. Loners are always hard to work with."

"Mike's different," Masterson replied. "First he's trying to get the last dollar squeezed out of the buffalo trade before the herds are gone. Then he plans to retire and settle down in Kansas City. He even has a widow woman lined up to marry. I'd give it a try, Slocum. There's a rendezvous in Buffalo Center later this month. If you don't connect with Shawnee Mike, you can find some kind of work."

"Rendezvous?"

"You know, a gathering of everyone in the buffalo trade," explained Masterson. "Just like those meetings up on the Green River in Wyoming back in the heyday of the beaver trade."

"Sounds interesting."

"All the whiskey sellers, cardsharps, whores, bunco artists, peddlers, and medicine shows will be there. Name your poison and chances are it'll be at Buffalo Center. Stop by the office in a few minutes," said Masterson. "I'll write a note recommending you to Shawnee Mike. It'll look better on official stationery."

A half hour later, John Slocum was on the trail heading toward Buffalo Center. The day was typical of the arid summer weather in western Kansas. The wind had started in the west shortly before dawn, gathering heat as the day wore on.

By the time Dodge City was a dot in the distance, the wind was like heated air forced from a devil's bellows. It carried heat from thousands of square miles of parched prairie. The wind was dry as lime.

John Slocum was uncomfortable riding in the heat. He kept a red bandanna tied loosely around his neck to soak up the sweat. Wavering heat waves shimmered on the horizon.

Riding along the trail, Slocum listened to the sounds of the plains. A man who survived on the frontier had to be a good listener. Every man heard the howl of wolves, the yap of coyotes, the bellow of bull buffalo, or the screech of an owl in the darkness.

But there were thin, tinier sounds that gave notice of what was happening in the grass and brush. The sprinting run of a prairie dog through the buffalo grass might be followed by the slithering sound of a rattlesnake. Or animals large and small scurried away from a rabid skunk, a prowling wolf, or a hungry wildcat.

Slocum had been a listener since his first pair of boots were given to him as a Christmas gift back in Calhoun County, Georgia. The boots enabled the young toddler to move beyond the family yard, to ramble the hollows and hills of the countryside.

Slocum's daddy said the boy should listen carefully when he left the yard. Listen for the sounds of rattlers, copperheads, and other vipers, Daddy said.

Listen for the distinctive sound of a poisonous water moccasin slithering across the surface of a creek. Listen for the sudden cracking of a twig, the stir of leaves, or the crackle of a foot or paw on dried moss. These sounds could be a warning of a two- or four-legged wild animal approaching.

In the Army, fighting for the Confederacy, Slocum's life depended on acute listening. The man who didn't pay attention walked into an ambush. A daydreaming soldier was a setup for Federal troops looking for a quick kill.

When he came west, Slocum made listening an automatic process—whether he was in a cow-town saloon, on the trail, or around a campfire. His ears picked up sounds, analyzed them, and filtered out those that did not suggest danger.

Now, on the trail to Buffalo Center, Slocum listened to the high-pitched hum of locusts. The insects' humming sound reminded him of the summer of his first visit to Savannah, Georgia. His daddy had to go there on business, so young John was allowed to accompany him. It was John's first journey outside Calhoun County.

The smells, sounds, and people of Savannah were a wonderment to the young man. The Yamacraw District of Savannah was crowded with black men—the enslaved working force of the city. They shaped the timbers, ran the forges, loaded the ships, and hauled the city's waste.

These Negro slaves carried bales of cotton and tobacco up the gangplanks of the tall-masted sailing ships. They scraped the barnacles off of the drydocked vessels. The back-straining labor in Savannah was performed by black slaves—under the supervision of white overseers.

The white bosses wore dapper coats, ruffled shirts, and boots polished to a gleaming black finish. They walked among the horse apples, mudholes, and crushed seashells used to fill the streets. They yelled out orders to the sweating slaves, then gathered in groups to passionately discuss the possibility of secession.

Crowds gathered to listen to speeches made by spell-binding orators. These wild-eyed zealots urged everyone in earshot to secede from the Union. These mesmerizers waved their arms as their harsh, insolent voices cried for the assassination of President Abraham Lincoln.

Later, swarms of locusts hummed as Slocum and his daddy hailed a carriage and rode off to visit the Savannah slave auction. John was surprised at the large crowd gathered for the sale. It was the largest gathering he'd ever witnessed.

The auctioneer was a gray-haired man in a white suit. He carried a straw hat with a bright red band, which he waved with his right hand to fan his face. Periodically, he pulled a white handkerchief from his coat pocket and wiped his brow.

The auctioneer stepped up on the platform beside the big stone auction block. He announced that the first batch of slaves were from a plantation in Louisiana. As he talked, two white overseers led a shackled slave from a holding pen. Slocum noticed that the big auction stone was worn smooth by the feet of men and women who had previously passed across the block.

The auctioneer's peppery spiel sang out the merits of the young black man.

"Looka this 'un! Strong shoulders! Yesiree! Friends, this buck has been trained to work. Starts at daylight and, by gum, never quits b'fore dark. He ain't never been branded, and the lash ain't touched his skin. This 'un is a docile buck. He's a prize because he's worked the forge and knows blacksmithin'. He'll make money for you. Save your money by havin' your mendin' jobs done at home. An' this buck'll earn money mendin' things for your neighbors. I'm not a-kiddin'."

Then the auctioneer began his chant as his ring men walked through the crowd crying for bids. Even then, Slocum knew that slavery was a corrupt, evil institution. The sale was his first contact with the sordid nature of slavery.

Like most smaller landowners in the South, the Slocums did not own slaves. Yet they and the other small farmers supported the right of large plantation owners to have slave workers.

Now, on the trail to Buffalo Center, Slocum's memories were interrupted by the sight of a white-topped covered wagon up ahead on the trail. The vehicle did not appear to be moving. Riding closer, Slocum saw that the left rear wheel was off the axle rim.

A florid-faced man with albino white hair came crawling from beneath the wagon. He placed a black top hat on his head and wiped his bare chest with a towel. He stood quietly and watched as Slocum approached.

Coming closer, Slocum saw that the man was in his middle fifties. He had a white mustache, heavily waxed, and had a genial smile on his face. His white shirt and dark blue frock coat were hung neatly on a hook on the right side of the wagon.

Slocum approached the stranded vehicle with caution. The left rear wheel from the wagon lay alongside the trail. Two spokes were broken. The wagon was held up by a long pole leveraged on two wooden boxes. The contents of the wagon were lying in the ditch. Boxes, wooden cases of bottles, and several feed sacks were stacked neatly in the buffalo grass.

A sign on the side of the wagon read:

DR. HOMER P. HOTCHKISS
Medicine for Humans and Animals
Creator of the Miraculous Mange Medicine
+ Salves to Destroy Fleas, Ticks, and Chiggers +
+ Indian Balms + Snakebite Oil + Celery Tonic +
+ Herbal Sachets + Madstones + Female Medicine +
+ Oriental Wax Balm + Wart Medicine +
A GUARANTEED CURE FOR EVERY AILMENT
OF MAN AND BEAST

As Slocum rode up to the wagon, the bare-chested man doffed his top hat. "Greetings, fellow traveler." The voice was warm and friendly. "I welcome you to the temporary abode of Dr. Homer P. Hotchkiss. I am the world-famous creator of a passel of pharmaceutical phenomena. I am the inventor of sensational salves, ineffable elixers, miraculous medicines, prodigious pills, and beneficial balms."

Slocum looked down from his saddle. "Doc, I'm not going to change your wheel."

"Pshaw! Perish such a thought," said the medicine man. "A young, strong man like yourself should not bend his back in a charitable act. No, kind sir, my back may be racked with age, my shoulders swollen with pain, but I never ask for assistance from a passing stranger. However, I would value your company while I change the wheel. Before I undertake the back-breaking job, I invite you to stop for a few minutes and share a dollop of whiskey with me."

Slocum swung down out of the saddle. He introduced himself and asked, "What caused the trouble?"

The doctor extended his hand. "Glad to make your acquaintance, Mr. Slocum. My first error, you see, was to trust a felon who pretended to be a wheel maker. The spokes shrank during this ungodly heat. The double-dealing miscreant used green wood to make the spokes. Fortunately, I always carry an extra wheel under the wagon bed. You never know, Mr. Slocum, when the dirty digit of destiny will diddle diligently in your affairs. I've learned to expect the unexpected. Experience has taught me to always eat the goose when the plate hits the table. Now, do you like your whiskey straight up or with a dash of Prickly Ash Bitters?"

Slocum waited as Dr. Hotchkiss went over to the ditch and rummaged in the wooden boxes. He returned with a bottle of premium Kentucky bourbon and two tumblers. He blew dust out of the glasses, wiped them with his shirt sleeve, and poured whiskey to the rim.

He handed one of the glasses to Slocum. "Sipping whiskey, sir."

"Thank you very much," Slocum said. He held his glass in a toasting position. "To your health."

Dr. Hotchkiss raised his glass. "May your hound dogs and horses be hearty, may your whiskey be old, may your cards all be high ones, and your women cute and bold."

They drank the contents of their glasses, and, with a gesture of goodwill, Dr. Hotchkiss lifted the bottle for refills.

As he poured, Dr. Hotchkiss asked, "What destination do you seek in this satanic wasteland?"

"I'm headed for Buffalo Center."

"My destination too," exclaimed Dr. Hotchkiss. "We are headed for a town of infamous sinners, pox carriers, drunkards, and unsavory characters. Dear sir, keep me company while I repair my wagon. Then we can sit topside on the wagon seat, enjoy our newfound friendship, and swap lies."

Slocum grinned. "Okay."

"Good!" Dr. Hotchkiss clapped his palms together. "Now, if you'll crawl under the wagon and lift out that wheel, we can get started."

Slocum sighed, crawled under the vehicle, and unloosened the bolts that held the replacement wheel. Meanwhile, Dr. Hotchkiss dug in his boxes until he found a container of axle grease.

Sweating in the late afternoon sun, they repaired the wagon. Next, the jack pole was eased off and the wagon dropped down onto the trail. Slocum helped reload the wagon with the doctor's supplies.

At last, Dr. Homer P. Hotchkiss surveyed his rig. "As good as new," he proclaimed. "My dear sir, you have sweated long and hard in my behalf."

Slocum's shirt was wet. A sticky dampness matted his hair. "I could use a good bath."

"About three miles west of here is a small creek that

never goes dry," said Dr. Hotchkiss. "There are a few trees for shade. A clean sandbar offers excellent camping. Plus, I have plenty of beans and salt-cured bacon for vittles. If you were to shoot a couple of prairie chickens we could dine like the fabled kings of yore."

Slocum's stomach howled for something to fill it. He agreed to ride ahead and shoot a few prairie chickens. He swung up into the saddle, pulled his rifle from the scabbard, and rode ahead of the slow-moving wagon, keeping an eye cocked for prairie chickens.

5

Slocum shot three prairie chickens, gathered kindling, and picked up an armload of buffalo chips. A fire was blazing by the time Dr. Hotchkiss pulled his medicine wagon up to the river crossing. Hotchkiss parked the vehicle on the sandbar, unharnessed his mules, and watered the animals. Slocum boiled water, doused the chickens, and plucked the feathers.

Once his animals were watered and hobbled, Hotchkiss sliced ample portions of bacon from a slab of salted pork belly. He fried the meat in an iron skillet shoved in the embers. When the bacon was crisped, he poured two cans of beans into the skillet. He added a cup of honey when the mixture started to bubble.

"Smells good," Slocum remarked.

Dr. Hotchkiss stirred the beans. "They're done. Time to dig in."

They talked about Buffalo Center while they ate.

"A rugged town," said Dr. Hotchkiss. "I was there for last year's rendezvous. Quite a shindig. Half a dozen men got shot. Most probably deserved it. A couple of dozen were knifed. And everyone was drunker than a hoot owl on a Christmas binge."

"Well, you're going back," commented Slocum. "You must've made money."

"I did."

"I hear buffalo men are spenders."

"They make money and love to get rid of it—fast."

Slocum asked, "Does your medicine work?"

"Better than most," Hotchkiss replied. "My mange medicine is pretty good. I got the recipe from a Kiowa medicine man. Now, tell me about yourself, Slocum. Were you in the war?"

Slocum became wary. "I don't like to refight old battles."

"Hell, I meant no offense," Hotchkiss said hastily. "One of my hobbies is telling a person's past by listening to their speech. You're from someplace in Georgia. Not a big city, but one of those little places in the backwoods. Right?"

"Calhoun County, Georgia."

"You were up north, probably during the war," Hotchkiss went on. "Virginia for sure, and you probably fought at Gettysburg."

"I was in both places."

"Thought so. It must've been hell."

After the parades, speeches, and recruitment drives in Calhoun County, Slocum and his brother, Robert, joined up. Slocum's group was commanded by Thomas Jonathan Jackson, a Scotch-Irish artillery officer from Virginia. Slocum admired the humorless colonel, who had served in the Mexican War and, later, taught at the Virginia Military Institute.

The test of Jackson's new troops occurred at the first battle of Bull Run. The Union army was expected to have an easy victory. No one in Washington, the nation's capital, was concerned about the clash of the two military forces.

Many wealthy thrill seekers from Washington rode out in their elegant carriages to witness the Federal troops whip the Southerners. They were dressed for an outing in the country. Their servants carried picnic baskets containing cold chicken, potato salad, and iced champagne to toast the victory.

The civilian onlookers discussed the war as if it was an athletic contest. Cannons boomed and rifles roared as the battle got under way. Jackson's brigade was at a pivotal point in the battle. His men held under the furious Federal assault, earning their commander the nickname of "Stonewall."

Under heavy fire, demoralized by heavy losses, frightened by the accuracy of Southern sharpshooters, the Federal troops panicked and retreated. Many dropped their weapons in their haste to rush from the battlefield. Others deserted their posts and stole horses to get away. The Washington socialites ran to their carriages and lashed their horses in a frantic effort to reach safety.

"I got my first taste of champagne that day," Slocum recalled. "A Yankee general had purchased fine French wine for a victory celebration. During the retreat, the rig overturned and smashed up in a creek. It was an awful scene. Dead bodies were everywhere. Corpses littered the banks of the creek. Men were dead in the water. Their blood had turned the water to a light pink color. But our group was wild with excitement, so we liberated the champagne and celebrated our victory."

"And the fact that you were alive," added Dr. Hotchkiss.

"That, too," agreed Slocum.

Following their victory at the first battle of Bull Run, Slocum became an infantryman in Stonewall Jackson's rugged campaign in Virginia's Shenandoah valley. Sometimes they marched thirty, forty—once, even fifty—miles

a day. Upon their arrival at their destination, the Rebels
fought like fresh troops.

"I learned victories are won by soldiers who never give
up," said Slocum. "Stonewall Jackson didn't know the
meaning of impossible. He was a great military genius. He
never considered defeat."

Jackson's army was pursued by superior Yankee forces.
Weaving, bobbing, moving in and out, hitting where the
enemy felt safest, Jackson's efforts helped the Southerners
maintain their gains.

After the second battle of Bull Run, Slocum was pro-
moted to corporal. He was placed in charge of a group of
sharpshooting snipers. Their mission was to assassinate
Yankee officers.

Slocum and his troops often spent a night lying in ambush, waiting for day to break over a Yankee encampment.
When the first rays of sun illuminated the enemy camp,
they aimed their Sharps carbines on their blue-coated tar-
gets. Once they made their shots, they scurried for safety
as Yankee cavalry pursued them.

By the time the two armies gathered for the battle of
Gettysburg, John Slocum was a cynical, battle-hardened
sergeant. His brother, Robert, a lieutenant, was killed at
Gettysburg. After that, John Slocum was numb and grief-
stricken, even though he was given a promotion for brav-
ery in battle.

Slocum interrupted his recitation about his war experi-
ences. He looked over at Dr. Hotchkiss. "I've been hog-
ging the conversation. How did you start telling a man's
history by how he speaks?"

"It was something to do while I traveled around. People
from different parts of the country use different words and
phrases. You add them to regional accents. Presto!" Here,
Hotchkiss snapped his fingers. "You learn how to judge a
man's background."

Slocum nodded. "Give me an example."

"Well, take Dodge City. That cow town is creating

words and phrases that are being carried to all parts of the country. You've been south of the line?" Hotchkiss referred to the wide-open part of Dodge City. This was where the town's brothels and crib joints were located. "They had a problem in Dodge City with drovers pounding on the doors of some family homes. First the city fathers decreed that all whorehouses had to be located across the railroad tracks. Pleasure palaces had to keep a red light in their windows. Even if you can't read, are dumb as a warthog, you can understand the symbol of a red lamp in a window. Now the people in Kansas City call their brothel neighborhood a red light district."

"Interesting," Slocum said. "Any other terms like that?"

"Get out of Dodge," answered Hotchkiss. "Drovers who drink up their pay say they're getting out of Dodge. That indicates they're moving on. Boot Hill is another term starting to catch on. That's the name of the original cemetery in Dodge City."

Slocum said, "Doc, you sure know a lot about things."

Hotchkiss chuckled appreciatively. "Nothing to gaining wisdom, my friend. You keep your mouth shut and your ears open. I think that's the procedure. I usually get it backwards. I always talked when I should have listened, to the detriment of my health and bank account. Have I told you about the time I was president of the Benevolent Society of Temperate Tipplers?"

"I'm glad to say you have not."

"It happened in St. Louis. A group of dowagers, nice society matrons with plenty of their husbands' cash, decided to clean up the town. My duty was to stroll through the pubs and saloons, delivering messages on the evils of John Barleycorn. Naturally, this provided ample opportunity to get paid for what I did most of the time for free. Unfortunately, the job ended when one of my sponsors saw me leaving a low-class joint in a state of intoxication. That is when I decided to get into medicine."

Slocum asked, "You went to medical school?"

"Hell, no," answered Hotchkiss. "I paid good money to a defrocked doctor, who signed and attested I'd studied medicine in his office for three years. Cost me three hundred dollars. But he also threw in a book on herbal cures and an illustrated guide on how to perform surgery."

"Did you practice in St. Louis?"

"Naw, I went to one of those itty-bitty mountain towns in Missouri. Practicing medicine was fairly easy there."

"I thought it required skill."

Hotchkiss poured another drink and slugged the liquid down. "Most cases were what I called either-ors. They either got well or they died. Take a farmer who gets kicked in the head by a mule. He's an either-or. Nothing can be done, even by the best doctor. So all I did was feed him whiskey until Mother Nature made her decision. Same method with gunshot wounds, most accidents, and childbirth. A doctor just stands back and lets Mother Nature take her course. The real problems in doctoring are the patients with vague complaints."

"What's that?" wondered Slocum.

"Well, my first experience was with a thin woman who looked like a scarecrow. Strictly a case of overwork, a lack of affection, and no sex."

Slocum laughed. "I knew we'd get around to where you started pronging your patients."

" 'Prescribe the medicine they need' was my motto."

Slocum looked skeptical. "That was her need?"

"Medicine is an art, not a science." Hotchkiss took another sip of whiskey. "A female patient comes into the doctor's office. She has complaints about vague aches and pains. In reality, she needs a pill to get rid of her husband. Unfortunately, we don't make them yet."

"What about poison?"

"A couple of times I've been close to prescribing it— for both husbands and wives."

Slocum grinned. "I'm glad I wasn't around when you were practicing."

Hotchkiss clear his throat and poured more whiskey. "You have to understand the female species. Those poor girls believed in fairy tales and princes, but what they usually married was a cross between an ogre and a miserly swineherd. Naturally, my practice was in a small Missouri town where gossip was rampant. Everyone talked about the smallest thing. The idea of a woman patient undressing for a physical examination was unheard of. The woman went behind a screen and then told me her complaints. I'm telling you the truth, Slocum, that's a hard way to examine someone. It's strictly by-golly and by-gosh checkups."

"How did you get past that?"

"To where I was screwing my patients?" Hotchkiss laughed. "I knew how to use herbs, poultices, patent medicines, and tonics. Shucks, I knew enough to suggest a man eat a lot of liver when he can't get an erection. Liver has something that toughens up the old dong."

"You're talking around the good part," said Slocum.

"Oh yeah, the women. This little scarecrow of a woman sort of seduced me. Her husband was an ambitious man working himself to death. Too pooped to pop when he finished working."

"Did she start it?"

"Hell, yes. The poor child just came walking around from behind the screen in her bare altogether. It didn't take a learned man to know what she needed."

"And you gave it to her?"

"Twice before her appointment was over."

"No complaints?"

Hotchkiss chuckled. "She made an appointment for the next week. The poor woman was just starved for sex, affection, whatever you want to call it. I feel that humanity needs a certain amount of skin-to-skin contact. Without it, we start getting these vague aches and pains. Our body organs lose their vitality. The blood thickens, and a person's constitution becomes morbid."

"I may take up medicine, Doc."

"A man with your handsome features and vitality could make a fortune."

"Let's get back to your first patient."

"Well, she'd never had an orgasm. Married for years, the mother of a couple of kids, and never once reached the Promised Land. I felt beholden to get her off—especially since an office visit cost a dollar."

"How'd you do it?" Slocum asked.

"I massaged her clitoris with my finger and tongue until she wrapped her thin legs around my neck!" Hotchkiss laughed, a wild barking sound. "The cure was remarkable, and after a few treatments she became docile in nature. The sourness of her facial features vanished. She was pleasant to be around."

"And you charged for each visit?"

"Son, you never forget money when doctoring. Else you'll end up on pauper's row."

"You don't believe in helping the sick and ailing?"

"If they've got a couple of dollars." Hotchkiss made a sweeping gesture with his hands. "Hell, I've treated some idiot who got hurt in an accident and didn't have a dime. They promised to pay, but forgot when they got well."

"Well, at least you had the women," Slocum remarked.

Hotchkiss sipped his bourbon. "They seemed to pass along the word by some secret grapevine. Women in town began to come into my office and ask for a treatment like Mrs. so-and-so is getting. Maybe they noticed the change in the disposition of my female patients."

"And you complied?"

Hotchkiss shrugged. He poured another glass of whiskey from the bottle. "Good deeds follow us into heaven, Mr. Slocum. My days were spent trying to calm the nerves of young, old, and unhappy widows, surly wives, single girls, and long-in-the-tooth spinsters."

"Each one had an itch?"

"My practice became scratching and stroking that itch. The widows had become accustomed to sex. The loss of their husbands created a void in their lives. Many of the married women had husbands who were like poppets—not puppets, mind you, but poppets. Pop on and pop on without any thought of pleasure for their partners."

Slocum grinned. "And we can't forget those sweet young ones without any experience."

Hotchkiss nodded with an expression of mock severity. "Never forget the young fillies who keep trying to guess what it is everyone is fussing over. Young unmarried women itched. God, they all seem to do that. But they're all afraid to have some lout scratch the offending part because of gossip. Same situation with spinsters. They need a man who is loving, has a degree of sexual finesse, and doesn't brag in taverns and pool halls about his conquests."

"How many were you handling a day?"

"Ah, I was younger then." Hotchkiss had a faraway glint in his eyes. "I could handle three, sometimes four patients."

"Why did you leave the town?"

"Mother Nature is a real prankster. Diddle enough women, and, despite precautions, a few will become impregnated with your seed. That happened in Missouri. A lot of women were birthing some healthy children—all with the same features. Their hair was as white as snow. Just like mine. And most of those infants looked just like me."

Slocum grinned with mock innocence. "Your children?"

Hotchkiss nodded. "There was gossip to that effect. It got tense tending to one of my sexual patients during childbirth. Relatives are gathered around for the blessed event. Invariably, we had a grandma who talked about how everyone in the family always had a small nose, small ears, and brown hair. Voilà! The mother produces a baby with my physical features and long, shaggy white hair. As you might surmise, suspicions began to grow in the minds of my patients' husbands. Pool hall operators were taking bets on who would shoot me. My troubles peaked when a couple of fathers-to-be joined in the betting."

"I'd say that was time to get out of Dodge."

"No one became violent," Hotchkiss went on. "There was talk, but nothing physical. One day I purchased a wagon and a good team. I hired a couple of louts, loaded up my equipment, and departed in the middle of the night. I sold the equipment in Kansas City, used the funds to create my medicine, and have moved from town to town since that time."

"A rolling stone gathers no moss."

"It also doesn't get shot by a jealous husband," said Dr. Homer Hotchkiss.

6

Slocum and Hotchkiss wanted to get an early start the next morning. While Slocum fed and watered the animals, Hotchkiss made cold sandwiches from leftover bacon. They were getting their animals ready for travel when a loud roar sounded across the river. An old buffalo came lumbering across the prairie through green grass that was knee-high on his front legs.

The old bull stopped on the bank across the river, raising his head and looking across the stream with his dim-sighted eyes. A pack of four wolves came moving through the grass behind the buffalo. The old bull was weak, too weak to fight off a pack of wolves. He stood still and lowered his head, and the wolves backed back away from his horns. The wolves respected the horns even though they were worn down to bony nubs.

Slocum walked over to his horse and started to pull his rifle from the scabbard. Then he was thoughtful for a moment and shoved the weapon back into the sheath. If he shot all of the wolves, another pack would soon come along to attack the old buffalo.

"Law of the plains," husked Dr. Hotchkiss. "The strong shall survive."

Slocum knew wolves followed and preyed on the buffalo, with foxes coming after the wolves, and rats, mice, and insects tailing the foxes. The mink killed the muskrat. The otter, wolverine, wolf, lynx, and bear killed each other and the beaver. The beaver, a placid little animal, only killed trees. Despite his passive nature, the beaver had been decimated by trappers crossing the rivers, plains, and mountains for his pelt. Every animal was prey to some other species.

The old buffalo lowered his head, swinging his horns at the circling wolves. It was apparent that he couldn't see the wolves. Buffalo are born with poor eyesight. Their eyes are dim at birth, and a shaggy forelock of hair adds to their blindness. Now, old and weak, the old bull was blindly fighting the wolves.

The big buffalo spun around when a wolf snapped at his back legs. Suddenly the bull gave a mighty bellow as one of his front legs sank into a muskrat hole. He twisted and jerked in a feverish effort to free his leg. Sensing victory and a feast, the wolves moved in with a swift attack, mouths open, teeth bared.

As the buffalo lunged and jerked, the wolf pack separated into two units. They came in on either side of the buffalo, sinking their sharp fangs into the old hide. They tore and ripped deeper into the flesh until the tendons were exposed. These cords were quickly gnawed in two. The old bull bellowed as he sank down on the riverbank.

"Not a pretty sight," Slocum remarked.

"I know." Chillbumps moved across Hotchkiss's skin.

The bull went down in the grass. Two of the wolves tore into the belly with feverish eagerness. The other two preda-

tors ripped deep into the old bull's haunches, coming away
with chunks of bloody meat.

The old bull was being torn apart, yet he rose up on his
spindly forelegs. His head rose up to the sky. Mighty bellows of anguish roared from his mouth. A wolf leaped at
the thick head matted with hair and came away with part of
the animal's lips.

"Shoot him," cried Hotchkiss. "Put the poor bastard out
of his misery."

"All right."

Slocum got his rifle and raised the gun, took careful
aim, and fired. The bullet tore into the animal's eye, then
smashed into the brain. With a moan, the old bull sank
slowly down into the grass. The wolves stood around the
dying buffalo, turning their bloody faces and staring across
the river. Their cold eyes measured the two men for an
instant, then they resumed their feast.

Later that morning, on the trail to Buffalo Center, they
encountered a band of Cheyenne Indians. The band consisted of eleven braves, about twenty squaws, and an equal
number of children. They were moving in a northerly direction, about a quarter mile south of the trail.

The braves were riding sturdy ponies that had grown fat
grazing on prairie grass. The Indians rode as if they had
been born on horseback. Slocum had seen Cheyenne children riding ponies before they could walk. The tribe was
noted for their feats of horsemanship and daredevil antics.

When the Indians spotted Slocum and Hotchkiss, they
kicked their ponies in the flanks and gave wild whoops.
They came pounding down upon the two men at breakneck
speed. Then, at the last instant, the Indians veered their
ponies away and went galloping past. They continued to
yell like banshees, racing to and fro across the rutted trail
and out into the grassy fields.

"Watch yourself," Slocum cautioned Hotchkiss.

"What tribe are they?"

"Cheyenne."

"You speak their tongue?"

"Fair," Slocum responded.

"Good," said Hotchkiss. "I don't want my white hair to decorate some Indian's spear."

Slocum and Hotchkiss reined to a halt on the trail. After several minutes of riding and yelling, the braves gathered in a circle around the two white men. They slid off the butts of their ponies, holding their shields and lances aloft, grinning with amusement.

The braves were armed with lances and bows and arrows, and two warriors carried flintlock muskets. The guns were old but in surprisingly good condition. The braves were pleased with their performance, proud of their horsemanship, and elated to have an audience.

· The chief remained behind his braves. When the other Indians dismounted, he kicked his pony in the flanks and came charging forward at a fast gallop. The pony picked up speed until it seemed as if both the chief and his pony would crash into Slocum's horse.

Then, with a triumphant cry, the chief yelled, pushed his hands down, and did a backward flip over the rump of his pony. He landed upright on his moccasined feet, rocked on his tiptoes for an instant, gained his balance, and stood before Slocum with a wide grin.

John Slocum did not change his expression. He looked at the bare-chested Cheyenne chief with a dead-pan expression, although he was impressed by the man's skill. Then Slocum turned his head and spat into the grass.

The chief's expression was one of joy and wild-eyed triumph. His braves raised their weapons above their heads, chanting a loud, guttural hymn to their chief's fighting ability. The bare-chested chief was dressed in leather leggings. He wore a beaded belt with an iron-headed Hudson's Bay Company tomahawk dangling in a short holster.

As his braves raised their voices to proclaim his prowess, the chief rippled the muscles of his arms and chest. Next he made a fist and beat his chest. He began to speak in a loud, singsong voice.

"What's he saying?" Hotchkiss wanted to know.

"He's telling about his conquests," Slocum answered. "Remember, this is a game to the Indians. They put on a show so that everyone knows they're lords of the earth. They love to have an audience."

Now the chief turned and faced his warriors. He moved his feathered, iron-tipped lance up and down in cadence with his words. Two scalps were tied to the end of his lance. One scalp was blond, the hair thin and matted, and Slocum wondered what the white man had done to end up with his hair on a Cheyenne spear.

The speech was almost poetic, a measured chant that brought a chorus of acclaim from the other braves. They grinned, stomped their feet, and pounded their chests. The Indians were like children in a schoolyard, impish with childish excitement. Slocum knew that playfulness had a dark side: it could turn to sadistic anger in an instant. He kept his hand close to his holstered pistol.

Slocum translated the chief's speech. "Doc, his name is Black Otter. He is the chief of this clan. They're Cheyenne and on a hunt for buffalo. He's the bravest Indian in the world, and his men are the finest warriors to ever go into battle. They can ride all day, chew up their enemies, and screw all night. Now, you'd better get ready for anything, because he's telling his braves that they're lucky to have found this wagon filled with whiskey."

At this point, the chief turned and looked directly at Slocum. "Whiskey," he said.

"No whiskey." Slocum spread his hands in a gesture of futility.

The chief pointed with his lance at Hotchkiss, who sat on the seat of the wagon holding a rifle. "Wagon got whiskey."

"No whiskey. Medicine," lied Slocum.

"Me see," said Black Otter.

The chief started walking toward the wagon. He hesitated at the sound of Hotchkiss cocking his rifle.

"Medicine," Slocum repeated. His hand moved closer to the butt of his holstered pistol.

The chief stopped, looked up at Homer Hotchkiss, and let loose a stream of insolent words. The braves listened intently, their heads cocked at a childish angle. Black Otter's eyes flashed with contempt as he shook his lance up and down with a steady tempo. At the end of his tirade, the chief slapped his groin with his open palm, then held his hand up in the air. His palm was opened toward Hotchkiss. The Indians roared with laughter.

Homer Hotchkiss reddened with embarrassment. "What's he saying to me?" he grumbled.

Slocum chuckled. "He claims your medicine is worse than the piss of a diseased buffalo cow."

Hotchkiss looked uncomfortable, and his face turned crimson. He nervously moved his hand through his mass of white hair. "I ought to shoot the sonafabitch," he said.

Black Otter moved away from the wagon and walked over to look up at Slocum. The man form Georgia slipped his boots out of the stirrups, ready to kick out if the chief made a threatening move.

Black Otter smiled. "We be friends. Forget whiskey."

Slocum grinned an acknowledgment.

"We wait for squaws, then ride with you for buffalo," Black Otter added.

In the end, the Indians became interesting traveling companions. The braves were like children playing king of the mountain. Everyone wanted to show off for the white men. They tried to outdo each other in feats of horsemanship. About an hour along the trail, the chief gave a low shout and pointed to a small herd of buffalo grazing in a field up ahead on the trail.

The braves galloped out for the kill. The herd consisted of about twenty-five bulls, cows, and calves. The Indians moved silently in and out of the herd in search of a striking point. Suddenly a brave saw an opening. His pony reacted instantly to the opportunity, spinning on his hooves as the Indian thrust his spear deep into the side of the animal, driving the weapon deep into the animal's lungs.

The speared animal sank slowly down to the ground. The squaws and children waited at the edge of the field. They gave a low sound of approval as the animal went down. Then the squaws were on their feet, rushing onto the field with their knives and tomahawks.

Their bronze faces held an expression of passionate hunger as they rushed to the downed beast. They plunged their knives and hatchets into the writhing body, drawing the blades out red and streaming with blood. Then, again and again, they hacked away at the struggling buffalo. Meanwhile, the braves were now spearing cows and calves with ease.

A young, slender Indian girl with a flawless face hurried across the field to join the squaws. She moved toward a calf that had been speared in the lungs. The small animal had a sleek black coat of fine hair that was reddening with blood.

The young Indian woman was armed with a long-bladed knife which she stabbed into the neck of the buffalo calf. The young buffalo dropped on its side and roared in a thin, high-pitched bellow.

The buffalo struggled to regain its footing. The calf's back haunches were down on the ground, but the animal's forepart rose up. The animal struggled up on its front legs. The head swung to and fro in a furious spasm of agony. Blood gushed from the calf's mouth and nostrils, a red stream that splattered the young squaw's buckskin dress.

She feinted with the knife, avoided the swinging head, and plunged the knife into the throat.

She stabbed continuously with the knife until her blade struck an artery near the calf's heart. Blood came rushing out in a red torrent, wetting her hands and spurting onto her garments. She stepped back as the calf wavered, legs shaky, eyes filmed over with a death glaze.

Slowly the little buffalo sank down into the knee-high grass as its lifeblood gushed out onto the green prairie grass. The head dropped to the ground as the girl's blade flashed into the animal's belly. The knife made a long slit as her bloody hands turned back the hide, exposing granite-gray fat on the belly.

The calf bellowed with pain as the flash of red meat appeared on the quivering underside. Feet and legs moving with spastic jerks, the buffalo tried to stand up. The Indian girl kept her distance from the jerking limbs and continued to turn back the hide on the belly.

She kept cutting into the inside of the buffalo until the intestines were exposed. Without opening a gut, her hand went in over the intestines and grabbed the liver. Without seeing the organ, she held it and slipped her knife in over the guts.

Then, holding a red strip of liver, she stood up and raised it to her mouth. She chewed and gulped down the first bite, then took another mouthful between her teeth. She brought up the knife and sliced this portion away and chewed furiously.

Slocum rode over to where the girl was standing. He swung down out of the saddle and stood looking at her. She looked so innocent even with the blood smeared over her face, in her hair, and on her eyelashes. Blood dripped from the front of her deerskin garments.

She looked at Slocum with shy amusement, raising one bloody eyebrow in a flirting motion. Then she turned and went back inside the buffalo's belly and sliced off another slab of liver. She brought this out and held it up for approval.

Slocum nodded his head, and she cut away a piece and placed the warm meat in his mouth. Slocum chewed the liver, and warm juices filled his mouth. He gulped down the meat. "Thanks," he said.

The girl did not acknowledge him, but went to the head
of the dying buffalo and pried open the jaws. She shoved
the knife past the teeth to the root of the black tongue.
With a quick twist of the knife, the Indian girl severed the
flesh and pulled out the moist tongue. She laid the tongue
on the fatty part of the animal's belly, then cut off two
pieces.

She shoved her slice of tongue into her blood-rimmed
mouth and handed the other piece to Slocum. He ate the
meat as the girl turned away and continued her butchery of
the animal. She made an incision down the inside of the
calf's leg, cutting the leg from ankle to flank, then began
to pull away the hide.

Slocum reached out to steady the leg when the buffalo
made a jerking motion. The Indian girl stopped working
and looked at him with puzzled eyes. Slocum recalled that
Indian squaws looked down on a man who did a woman's
work. He drew his hand away from the leg, thanked the
squaw for the meat, and wiped his hands on the soft hair of
the calf's head. Then he walked back to his horse and
swung up into the saddle.

The Indian braves had killed several animals, then allowed the rest of the herd to move away. The braves had
left the field and were gathered at their campsite. They sat
and watched as the squaws butchered the fallen buffalo.

Slocum rode over and raised his hand in a gesture of
goodbye.

Black Otter walked up and expressed his disappoint-
ment at Slocum's departure. "Eat all night. Play with
squaws," he said.

Slocum looked over at the young Indian girl and wondered about her prowess as a lover. Then he thought about
the whiskey in the medicine wagon and the possibly high
alcohol content of the patent medicines. One of the braves
would be curious, and that could lead to problems. It was
best to move on to Buffalo Center.

"We have to get to town," Slocum told Black Otter.

"Come visit the people," the chief invited. He raised his hand and pointed to the southwest. He gave directions to his home camp in a singsong, gesturing with his hands and stabbing the air with his fingers.

"I may do that someday," Slocum said.

"You see white boss?" asked Black Otter.

"I might."

"Tell white men to stop killing buffalo," said the Indian chief. He gestured with his arm in a sweeping motion. "Too few buffalo. Too many killed. Buffalo go, and Indians have nothing to eat. Indians starve."

"I'll tell them," Slocum promised.

The Cheyenne chief stood with crossed arms as Slocum crossed the field and rode back to the trail. Homer Hotchkiss waited beside his rig. The medicine man crawled up on the wagon seat, yelled to his mules, and they headed toward Buffalo Center.

7

The two companions rode until Buffalo Center came into sight. On the outskirts of town they came to a dirty tent erected beside the trail. A large keg of whiskey rested on two sawhorses in front of the makeshift saloon.

A thin man with a pockmarked face came rushing out of the tent as the wagon approached. "Come in, pilgrims," the shill smiled crookedly. "Have a free drink on me."

Hotchkiss raised his white eyebrows. "Good whiskey?"

The pockmarked man's gaze swept over the medicine wagon. An expression of greed came over his face. "Kentucky prime," he lied. "The first cup is free. Come and visit with me. I got a nice friendly woman who's getting out of bed to meet you-all."

"Thank you kindly," Slocum responded. "I've got to ride on into town."

Hotchkiss looked down at the pockmarked man. "Thank

you, sir, for your splendid offer. However, I treasure my innards and never touch rotgut."

A horse-faced woman in a dirty red dress came staggering out of the tent. Her hair was disheveled, and her face and mouth were slack with drunkenness.

The whiskey seller cursed as the two men moved past the whiskey tent. "Go on back inside!" he roared at the woman. "You done scared 'em off. I told you to be ready for the live ones!"

Buffalo Center was a mishmash of clapboard shacks, saloons, brothels, gambling halls, a ramshackle wooden hotel, several general stores, and a dozen small specialty shops.

Ringing the business district were a wheel and wagon repairman's shop, a gunsmith, several cafes, a boarding-house, and a smithy.

The tinny sound of out-of-tune pianos came from the saloons. A half-dozen frontiersmen in buckskins staggered along the muddy street. A group of drunken men argued in front of the batwing doors of an unpainted clapboard saloon.

Thousands of buffalo hides dried to a flinty hardness were stacked in vacant lots. Wagons loaded with hides were lined up along the side streets. Several large wagons with tall rick sides were parked in an alley. These wagons were ready to be pulled to Dodge City, where the hides would be loaded onto railcars and shipped east.

The most impressive building in Buffalo Center was a large, sprawling livery stable with an attached corral. Slocum reined in his horse and slid down out of the saddle by the hitching post.

A short, pudgy man in homespun trousers and shirt came out of the gloominess in the building. "Welcome to Buffalo Center," he said, extending his hand. "I'm George Lewis. Costs twenty cents a day to stable your horse. That includes feed, tender loving care, and any attention the animal may need. I like dumb things, which is why I got married, and I'll be good to your horse."

Slocum accepted the offer, shook the man's hand, and introduced himself.

George Lewis started to say something when he looked over Slocum's shoulder. His face brightened at the sight of the medicine wagon. He let loose with a war whoop. "Doc!" screamed Lewis. "Dangnation! You made it!"

Homer Hotchkiss pulled up in his white-topped wagon and stepped down from the seat. He grabbed the liveryman's hand and slapped him on the shoulders. They exchanged loud statements of friendship.

"George, you want to care for my wagon and team?" Hotchkiss asked.

"I'd be upset if anyone else got the job," answered Lewis. "Now, Doc, you set the brakes on your wagon. Slocum, tie your nag to the hitching post. You gents come inside and I'll open up some soda pop. Got strawberry or sarsaparilla. Take your pick."

Slocum and Hotchkiss followed the fat man into the building. They went into a large office furnished with an oak rolltop desk, chairs, and a horsehair sofa. Lewis waved his hand for his guests to take a seat.

He waddled over to a corner and pulled the burlap covering from a small wooden box. His fat fingers plucked three bottles of soda pop from the cool interior. "It'll have to be strawberry," he said. "Only flavor left. Those kids of mine raided my soda-pop cache when I wasn't looking."

"George has eleven kids," Dr. Hotchkiss informed Slocum.

"Twelve now, Doc," said Lewis, coming across the room. "You've been gone a year. My woman—Lettie's her name, a wonderful woman even if she is slow upstairs—likes children. Lord knows, we been blessed with a few more than our share. Lettie keeps wondering how she keeps knocked up. I don't have the heart to tell her because she likes fiddle-faddling so much. If you got a woman who likes screwing, I figure that's as close to heaven as you're going to get in this vale of tears. Besides, Lettie likes babies and children."

George Lewis smiled as the two men accepted their bottles of strawberry soda pop.

"George is famous for his soda making," said Hotchkiss.

"Enjoy, gents. It's home-brewed and as tasty as I can make it."

Slocum took a sip and complimented the fat livery stable owner on his soda-making skills.

The liveryman beamed with pleasure. "You going to be here for a while?" he asked.

"Maybe."

"Stop by anytime," Lewis said. "I'll always have a bottle of soda pop for a man who enjoys it."

"Thanks for the invitation. Right now I'm looking for a gent named Shawnee Mike Samuelson," said Slocum.

"Comes to town every evening about this time," answered Lewis. "He brings in meat to the butcher shop. Fresh-killed buffalo. Folks in Buffalo Center like their buffalo meat. Although once in a while I get tired of the taste. That's why Lettie and me got a flock of chickens. I also keep my older kids out on the river fishing. Nothing like a good bullhead or catfish fried up nice and crisp. Now, do you know Samuelson?"

"Heard about him," Slocum replied.

"He's a hard man, like most beaver men," Lewis went on. His voice was mild and conversational. "Mike can be cranky at times, but overall he's a fair man."

"How's he to work for?"

"His boys got no complaints," said Lewis. "They're making good money."

"Where do I find him?"

"He'll be over at the Hunters and Hiders Saloon about sundown." Lewis took another swig from his bottle of soda. "Look for a big red Studebaker wagon out in front.

That's the only kind of wagon Mike will buy. I get them for him out of Kansas City. Costs a little more, but Mike figures the extra quality is worth the price. Maybe it is."

"What about the big shindig this year?" asked Dr. Hotchkiss. "I figured it would be starting about now."

"Maybe in another couple weeks," Lewis said. "Folks are thinking of canceling it."

Hotchkiss's white eyebrows popped up. He looked at the liveryman with a surprised expression. "I come a couple hundred miles for this rendezvous. I got a wagonload of medicine to sell."

Lewis gestured with his fat palm. "Easy, Doc, don't get your liver churning. The big herd of buffalo is about ten miles north of town. Hunters and hiders ain't taking time off for anything. They're killing and skinning from daylight to dark. We'll have the rendezvous, all right, but it'll be a couple of weeks later than last year."

Hotchkiss pursed his lips. "Well, they ought to have plenty of money."

"Money?" Lewis drained the last soda from his bottle. "All those jaspers got is money, mosquito bites, fleas, and ticks. Don't worry, you'll sell every bottle of medicine in your wagon. Now, Mr. Slocum"—Lewis smiled at the man from Georgia—"if you want to catch Shawnee Mike, you'd better get over to the saloon. Mike will be pulling his wagon in there before much time passes."

Slocum left Hotchkiss and Lewis talking in the office of the livery stable. He walked out into the twilight and looked up and down the street. The Hunters and Hiders Saloon was a rough wooden building with a crudely painted sign in front.

Slocum crossed the rutted main street and went through the batwing doors. The stench of sweat, beer, whiskey, and unbathed men assailed his nostrils.

A dozen men in bloodstained homespun or buckskins stood at the crude bar. They were a tough-looking group with unkept beards, long hair, and suntanned faces. Every man wore a gunbelt with a pistol on one hip, a bowie or Hudson's Bay knife on the other side.

A tall, thin man in a dirty white shirt was serving drinks at the far end of the rough bar. He worked with a slow, haphazard motion that indicated he was slightly drunk or was working off a monstrous hangover.

Several minutes passed without the bartender coming to take Slocum's order, and he was about to leave the saloon and stand in front until Shawnee Mike Samuelson showed up when the batwing doors of the saloon swung open and a fancily dressed young woman walked into the room. She was short with a petite figure.

The male customers began to hoot and holler as the woman walked into the smoke-filled saloon. She walked with a sexy, self-confident strut. She had brownish-blond hair, an attractive face, full lips, and an hourglass figure under her blue velvet gown.

"Howdy, Pearl!" cried a paunch-bellied old man, pushing back his chair and weaving by a table.

"Howdy yourself, Caleb!" The woman had a strong, sexy voice. "I see you've got an early start on tonight's drunk."

"Dern right!" The old man smiled with pleasure at the recognition from the woman.

"Pearl! You gonna sing tonight?" squawked another customer.

"Later on, maybe, later on!" said the woman in a lilting voice.

"We'll take that as a promise," husked a wild-looking man with a bandage around his head.

"You got it!"

The young woman stepped behind the bar, picked up two empty tin cups, and placed them in a metal washbasin. Still smiling, she came over and stood across the bar from Slocum. "What's your choice, mister?" she asked in a pleasant voice.

Slocum smiled. "You'd slap me if I told you."

She answered quickly, "Beer or whiskey?"

"Beer."

"Regular stuff costs a nickle and its rotgut," said the woman. "I got a few bottles of St. Louis brew for a dime. Pick your poison."

Slocum laid a dime on the bar. "Thanks for the advice. Is your name Pearl?"

"Pearl Buckley," the woman replied, looking up into Slocum's face. "I own the joint. It ain't much, mister, but it'll do until I find something better."

The young woman walked to the middle of the bar. She returned with a thick glass mug and a bottle of St. Louis premium beer. She nodded cordially at Slocum, picked up the dime, and said, "Help yourself to the free lunch. The boiled eggs are fresh. Eat all you want."

Slocum poured his drink and sipped the foamy liquid. The beer was a tasty concoction with a thick flavor of hops. It was much better than the stale beer sold in most frontier towns.

The young woman set three boiled eggs on the counter in front of Slocum. "Throw the shells on the floor," she advised. "Housekeeping in Buffalo Center is a rare commodity. I tried keeping the place neat and tidy, but these bozos are dirtier than the animals they kill. You're new in town, right?"

"Just got in."

"Welcome to the rectum of the frontier," said Pearl Buckley.

"Is it that bad?"

She looked up into Slocum's eyes. "Depends on the company."

"You ought to have your pick." Slocum jerked his thumb toward the room filled with male customers.

"A girl could do that," Pearl admitted. "But I don't see anyone worth trying."

The woman turned her head to check out the bar. When

she moved, the top of the blue velvet dress slipped down, exposing the tops of her breasts.

As she pulled up the bodice of the low-cut dress, she noticed that Slocum's gaze was fixed on her ample breasts. "I'm not advertising! I paid good money for this dress in Kansas City, and the dang thing won't stay up."

"My compliments to the tailor." Slocum raised his drink, smiling.

"I gotta help Jeb tend bar," the woman said. "He ain't much, but he's dependable. He drinks too much, but so does everyone out here. Mainly, he stays in town and shows up for work every day. He doesn't get crazed and chase buffalo like the rest of these yahoos."

Slocum asked, "Is Shawnee Mike Samuelson around tonight?"

Pearl Buckley shook her head. "Not yet. You a friend?"

"Yep."

"I'll let you know when he comes in."

Saying this, Pearl Buckley moved down the bar as the patrons smiled or grimaced for her attention.

Slocum looked around the saloon. More customers were coming into the establishment, entering through the back door. Most of the patrons were intent on getting drunk. That was their privilege, and as long as no one gave him any trouble, Slocum gave them plenty of room.

Slocum cracked and peeled the boiled eggs, ate slowly, and sipped the beer. He kept his gaze on Pearl Buckley's attractive figure, wondering how she would be as a bed partner. He liked small women, enjoying being in bed with their heads lying on his chest.

Occasionally Slocum glanced out toward the street, looking for some sign of Shawnee Mike Samuelson. It was growing dark when a red Studebaker wagon pulled up in front of the saloon. A wiry little man in buckskins set the brake on the rig, jumped down, and walked inside. His suntanned face was as dry as a piece of worn leather. His dark eyes were deep-set under bushy black brows.

The old man's greasy gray hair was combed straight back and knotted in a ponytail. A salt-and-pepper beard hid the lower part of his face. A large old high-crowned beaver hat was perched on his head at a cocky angle.

Pearl Buckley hurried up as the little man came up to the bar.

"Evenin', Pearl. Gimme one of those beers," said the little man, pointing to Slocum's bottle.

Pearl Buckley brought the beer. "This is Shawnee Mike," she said to Slocum.

The little man looked at Slocum with a suspicious glance. "You lawman or bill collector?" he asked.

"Neither. I'm looking for a job. I heard in Dodge City you're looking for a man who can shoot and hit something."

"Could be," replied Samuelson in a noncommittal tone. "Who told you to look me up?"

"Bat Masterson."

"You know Bat?" Samuelson ignored the mug and took a long guzzle of beer from the bottle. He wiped his mouth with a leather sleeve. A suspicious glint flickered in his dark eyes. "What's Bat look like?"

"Same as ever. All duded up." Slocum pulled the letter written by Masterson from his pocket. "He wrote this to you."

Samuelson took the letter. He squinted his eyes and peered in the dim light at the paper. Then he laid the sheet on the bar, raised the bottle to his lips, and drained it.

"What's it say?" asked Samuelson. "I ain't too good at reading. Never took time to learn that art. Left home before my ma could get any school teaching done on me. Come to think about it, you shouldn't read it. You got an interest in it. Hey, Pearl! Come over here, honey, and read this letter for me."

The young woman came over, picked up the paper, and held it up to catch the light from a flickering oil lamp.

"It's from the marshal's office in Dodge City. 'Dear

Shawnee Mike,'" she read. "'This is John Slocum, a good man with a gun—pistol, rifle, or shotgun. He'll make you a good hunter.' And it's signed by William Barclay Masterson."

Pearl Buckley laid the letter on the bar and went off to fix a drink for a grumbling customer at the end of the bar.

Shawnee Mike watched the movement of her hips with an appreciative eye. "So you're a sharpshooter, eh? Think you could hit the target on that?" asked the little man. He looked at Slocum with a genial expression.

"I usually hit what I aim at."

"Makes me want to be young again." Samuelson said. "Now, I know Bat Masterson wouldn't stand up for some trail bum. You ever hunted buffalo?"

"Just for my own meat."

"Where you from?"

"Here and there."

"Any posters out on you?"

"Not lately."

"Good. I ain't got nothing 'gainst outlaws," Samuelson said. "I just don't like lawmen or Pinkerton detectives snooping round my camp. They'll upset every man in camp. And it gives me a case of the willies too. You ever handle a Sharps buffalo gun?"

"I've never even seen one."

Samuelson yelled for another beer. Pearl Buckley came over and slammed the bottle down with a *thunk*.

The old man laughed and took a long swig from the bottle. "Never did know why women get highfalutin when you yell for service. That's why they've been put on earth." He belched. "Now, these Sharps guns are something new. Deadly as hell on buffalo because it throws a .50-caliber piece of lead. Takes 140 grains of powder per round, and the slug weighs in at 750 grains."

Slocum grinned. "What size wheels does it have?"

The old man slapped his hand on the bar. "By cracky,

that's good! It could use wheels, all right. I use a tripod mount. Else the kick would tear off your shoulder."

The old man took another drink of his beer. He looked around the dimly lit saloon and laughed. Slocum liked him, even if there seemed to be an edge underneath the smile.

"I enjoy coming into town," Samuelson said. "Nothing better than watching people get drunk. I got tired of the wilderness a long while back. Humans ain't born to be loners. We're herd animals just like the buffalo."

"You must've had the tribes to visit with," Slocum said.

"A man gets tired of Indians if he has any sense," said Samuelson. "Their interests are mighty limited. Like who shot the last bear and why the other tribes are bastards. Anyhow, you looking for work?"

"Can you use another hunter?" Slocum asked.

The old man was thoughtful, rubbing his thumb over the neck of his beer bottle. His dark eyes focused on Pearl Buckley's swaying hips as she moved back and forth behind the bar.

"Reckon we might make a deal," he said at last. "I got wagons for hauling hides and a fancy chuck wagon out at camp. My crew includes a couple of skinners, a cook, and four men for curing and dressing the hides. You know about that?"

"I don't."

Samuelson chuckled. "Figured you might be slim in that area. Tell you what. Spend a couple days with me and I'll pay a buck a head for every head you shoot. If things work out, then we can look to a long-term situation. I'd like to get back to Kansas City for a couple of weeks. I've been sparking a widow lady back there. She's richer'n King Midas, believe you me, and I'm overdue back there. A man can get too busy. Some other jaybird will come along and steal my woman. Me? I can't think of anything better'n snuggling up to a rich widow in my old age. Maybe I can sneak in some practice if you run the crew."

"I don't have enough experience to ramrod," Slocum said.

Samuelson looked amused. "You had anything to do with widow women?"

Slocum shrugged. "I've run across a couple down the trail."

"Then I'll stay here and you go goose the widow!" Samuelson laughed. He held his hand out, palm up. "Second thought, any goosing gets done, I'll do it."

"Fair enough."

"Like most things in life, hunting buffalo has a few tricks to it." Samuelson sipped his beer. "I learned mine the hard way. I'm willing to pass them along to you. That agreeable?"

Slocum raised his beer mug. "Sure is."

Samuelson clicked his bottle against Slocum's mug. His voice was jubilant. "Here's to us!"

They drank their beer and waved a farewell to Pearl Buckley.

Slocum followed the old man out of the saloon.

"Don't get any ideas about that gal," the old man said, pushing through the doorway.

"She looks appealing," Slocum admitted.

"Pearl doesn't mess with men."

"You can't be killed for trying."

The old man stopped beside his handsome red wagon. "Listen, Slocum. She does not screw. Got that? I seen men do everything except kill themselves. Pearl won't mess around. She takes one man and the rest of her customers would get bent out of shape. Save your breath and gonads."

"Okay." Slocum smiled.

"I got to deliver my load of meat." Samuelson crawled up on his wagon. "I hate seeing meat spoiling out in the country. My boys fill up the wagon every day with prime buffalo pieces. Gives me an excuse to come into town and be with people. 'Sides that, this dumb German butcher gives me six cents a pound for it. I make a profit and get my beer, too!"

"I'll get my horse," Slocum said.

Samuelson shook the reins. The team of mules moved out slowly. "I'll be behind the meat market in the next block," said the old man. "Meet me there and we'll go out to camp."

Slocum crossed the street to the livery stable. His horse was standing where he had tied the animal to the hitching rack. Homer Hotchkiss and George Lewis were inside the office, talking. Slocum watered his animal, picked up a bag of oats, and told the two men he was leaving.

He swung up into the saddle and rode into the alley. Lantern light flickered through the open doorway of a tar-paper-and-canvas building. The last of the buffalo meat was being unloaded from Shawnee Mike's bright red wagon. Coming closer, Slocum glanced inside at two rough-hewn tables covered with hump meat, tongues, livers, and shank cuts.

The butcher was a stocky, big-shouldered man. His butcher's apron and Shawnee Mike's leathers were stained with blood. Flies and gnats buzzed around the two men and the meat on the table.

Shawnee Mike came out of the building. "Well, we better get moving," he said, crawling onto the wagon seat.

The butcher stood beside the ramshackle building and nodded as Slocum and Shawnee Mike rode off down the alley.

8

Shawnee Mike Samuelson's camp was located on a hillock overlooking a small stream four miles north of Buffalo Center. The crew was sleeping when Slocum and the old man rode into camp. They hobbled their animals and walked up the hillock to the camp. A small clump of embers glowed under an iron pot on a tripod near the chuck wagon. Shawnee Mike stirred the embers, and, by the golden light, Slocum spread out his bedroll and went to sleep.

The camp was roused the next morning by the clang of a cook's ladle against an iron triangle. Slocum rubbed sleep from his eyes as Shawnee Mike introduced the other members of the crew. They were rough, weary men with strong body odors. They mumbled their greetings to Slocum, then went off to the creek to wash the sleep from their eyes.

After a quick breakfast, the other men went to work out on the plains. The little old man and Slocum remained in camp. Samuelson crawled up into a supply wagon covered with a canvas top and came back down with a large-bored gun.

"This is the Sharps fifty," he said. "Some call it the shoot-today, hit-tomorrow gun. Be careful, because she's heavier than you expect."

Slocum took the gun, and his hand dropped slightly from the unexpected weight. "This is a real cannon," he said.

"Wait till you use it! She's a beauty!" Samuelson handed the rifle tripod to Slocum.

They saddled their horses and rode out on the prairie. Samuelson was in a talkative mood. The little old man liked being around people, especially people willing to listen.

"A lot of folks have the wrong idea about buffalo," Samuelson said. "They're filthy critters. Maybe not because they want to be, but because of their nature. They get to be a real pest in the springtime when they're shedding hair. They itch and burn and go crazy trying to find a big rock or a tree to rub up against. Lord, nothing smells as bad as that old buffalo matting. Old dead hair caked with mud, sweat, vermin, and scabs. I feel sorry for those poor critters. After they get the old hair rubbed off they've got these hairless, bald areas that are usually bleeding and tender. That's when the flies move in."

"I've seen crazed old bulls running across the plains," Slocum said.

"Yep. They're more than likely trying to get away from the horseflies that are the size of a man's thumb. Sometimes bigger. Some folks call them bulldog flies. They got a helluva bite, as you know, and they don't quit feeding until their gut is full."

"Don't forget the ticks."

Samuelson nodded. "By the millions. Think of ticks dug

into your skin so deep that you can't rub them off. Rub away the body and the head stays lodged in your skin. Then, add the fleas, wood lice, deer flies, mosquitos, gnats, and all the other the pests. Buffalo got a hard life. You ever run into skeeter that was real big? I mean, turkey buzzard size?"

"Down in south Texas," Slocum replied. "We sat up the whole night choking in smoke. A hot summer night. We had to build fires to keep the mosquitos away."

"At least a man has hands for swatting them," the old man went on. "The buffalo, poor bastards, can't do anything. They're also half blind. They're dim-sighted at birth. Then they get that forelock of hair on their head hanging over their eyes. That carries hordes of insects that feed on their eyes or crawl all over the rims."

"Never thought of a buffalo like that."

"And if it ain't flying pests eating them alive," Samuelson went on, "the poor devils got the hot summer sun blistering their naked skin. Where they shed their winter hair, I mean. Then the crows, magpies, and ravens figure out all the flying and crawling insects travel on the buffalo. So those birds come perch on his poor back, pecking and driving the buffalo into a frenzy. I've seen them go bellowing off like mad animals, or else they find a mudhole and roll and wallow till their bodies are covered with mud."

"Don't forget prairie fires," Slocum said. "I've seen them with their hair burned off, their eyes burned out, and maybe fifty of them staggering around. They were falling into ravines, bumping into trees, and wandering around like lost souls. Indians set that fire."

"Indians ain't very noble with the buffalo." Samuelson spat. "Course, there's always something after the buffalo. Floods get them too. I was up north where the Canadian herds roam. A stampede got started, maybe set up by the Indians or a flash of lightning or something. Thousands of buffalo stampeded into a river. So many carcasses that they formed a dam. Stopped the river from flowing and drove it over the banks. And the squaws were out crawling over those dead buffalo to cut out the liver and tongues. Now, you ever watch the bulls fight?"

"Used to."

"I come to the wilderness as a tad of a boy," said Samuelson. "Green as spring grass. First time I saw two bulls go at it, I thought those two monsters would kill themselves. It was rutting season, and they were fighting over cows. They'd bellow loud enough to shake the ground. The snot and goop shot out of their nostrils by the bucketfuls. God, what a sight! Their flanks were heaving, their heads lowered, and they rushed at each other, skull on skull. They hit with such power you could hear the crash of their hitting a mile away. Funny thing is, with all that snorting, bellowing, and head bashing I never saw one bull get hurt by another one. I used to think they didn't have brains, but they do."

A half mile from the camp Samuelson reined in his horse and sniffed the air. "A small herd is up ahead."

They rode for a few hundred yards up a gradually sloping rise of land. They came to the top of a high mound and looked down onto the Kansas prairie. About eighty bulls, cows, and calves grazed in a flat meadow. Another dozen animals were scattered along both sides of a small, muddy stream. One old bull buffalo wallowed in a low spot where the creek sloshed out of the normal channel. He rolled to and fro on his back, kicking his legs in the air.

The animals were ridiculous in appearance. Most of a buffalo—about eighty percent of its weight and bulk—was forward from the penis sheath. The flesh rose to a huge, useless hump along the shoulders and around a large, powerful neck and head. The head was decorated with two small little horns that protruded like two tusks from the animal's skull.

The forward part of the body was covered with long, thickly matted hair. Back from the middle, the hair was a short fuzzy nap. Equally ridiculous were the small rear flanks: tiny legs and thighs with the huge pouch of testicles dangling between them. The bag bounced back and forth whenever a bull moved.

The animal's tail was a short, useless ornament. The small hooves seemed too small for the great weight. Their feet slashed narrow trenches into the prairie topsoil, six to eight inches deep wherever they stepped.

"Gold on the hoof," said Shawnee Mike. "Never figured I'd see the day when buffalo hides were worth four dollars apiece. Figured the only thing buffalo hide was good for was a robe. The buyers don't care whether the hair is prime or not. Folks back east use them for buggy tops, bookbindings, and furniture and wall coverings. You know about the steam engines?"

"I've seen them."

"Well, a buffalo hide makes the best belt in creation for a steam engine. You probably know 'bout as much as I do about hunting buffalo. But I'll go over things to be sure. First you bring down the leader of the herd with your first shot. He's your first target. Leave him and the old bull may be smart enough to start the whole herd running away."

"How do you tell the lead bull?" asked Slocum. He figured spotting the leader was the same as picking the head steer in a batch of cattle.

"Gut feeling."

"Nothing else?"

"It ain't something you can put into words. You either have the knack of figuring out the leader or you don't make a shooter." Shawnee Mike sniffed the wind again. "Most folks think good shooting is all you need, but that's just part of it. The lead bull should come down first. Go for a lung shot and they'll drop right over. Shoot a slug in the heart and they'll run maybe three to four hundred yards, gushing blood by the buckets. That'll get the herd upset, and off they got lickety-split. Skinners can't work fast if they're running all over the country to reach the carcass.

So keep the ones you bring down in as small an area as possible."

"How would you handle this herd?" Slocum wondered.

"I'd move in close and drop the leader," answered Shawnee Mike. "He's the big one off to the north with the dried mud on his hind flank. I'd get downwind, which don't count for much, because buffalo can't smell worth a dang. Sometimes, though, they pay attention and something will spook them. So work with the wind blowing away from the herd."

"Sounds easy enough."

Shawnee Mike cupped his hands and lit his cigar. "Once you get the leader, then you keep right on shooting. Get all you can as fast as possible. A man never knows about buffalo, so you shoot when they're in your sights."

"How many would you get out of a herd like this?"

"Forty or fifty head."

"In how big an area?"

"Maybe a quarter mile. I keep things neat and easy for the skinners."

"The gunfire ever cause a stampede?"

"Not often, because they're dim-witted," answered the old man. He explained that a good hunter never started shooting until the sun was high in the sky. "Around ten o'clock is best," he said. "Buffalo are just like folks. They get up in the morning, shake the sleep out of their heads, trot off to the creek for a drink of water. The herd is spread out all over the countryside. They got to pass gas, nibble a little grass for breakfast, and do their business. I wait until the roaming around is over and they're clumped together for some serious grazing. I drop them right beside each other instead of spreading the bodies out."

After dismounting, Slocum pulled down the Sharps rifle and tripod. Both pieces of equipment were in leather cases. Samuelson pulled a canvas water bag off his saddle horn. They went down the slope toward the herd of buffalo. The animals were in a tight group. A couple of bulls were off from the herd, grazing a quarter of a mile away.

Slocum wet his finger and tested the direction of the wind. Then he found a level spot and set the tripod in the grass. Next he placed the rifle on the tripod and loaded the gun. He lay down on his belly and turned the gun in the direction of the herd.

"Watch the kick," cautioned Samuelson.

Slocum took aim at the lead buffalo's chest. Slowly he squeezed the trigger. The big-bored rifle boomed, and orange flame shot out of the barrel. Simultaneously, the acrid smell of gunpowder polluted the clean prairie air.

The heavy slug struck the big bull in the lungs. The animal was driven back a step by the power of the bullet. Then the front feet pawed the earth for a moment and the big body trembled. The buffalo stood there, seemingly suspended in place, and then with a feeble moaning noise dropped over into the tall prairie grass.

"Keep shooting," Samuelson said. He picked up the canvas water bag. "I'll pour on water to keep the barrel cool."

Slocum slipped another cartridge into the chamber. He took aim and fired at a cow standing near the fallen bull.

The gun boomed again, and the animal went down.

Again and again Slocum aimed and fired the gun. The kick from the Sharps was a vicious, ugly snap that pulled the gun and tripod up off the ground. The mechanism moved back about six inches with each shot.

Slocum continued to shoot the breech-loaded gun. The barrel of the gun was heating up from the fast shooting.

"Keep shooting," Shawnee Mike said. He lifted the canvas bag and poured water over the barrel. The metal hissed, and for an instant Slocum thought steam might rise up from the barrel. He inserted another cartridge, took aim, and another buffalo was struck by the heavy lead slug.

Samuelson poured more water on the gun barrel, then

stood up and counted the carcasses. "Eighteen," he said. "Keep going."

Slocum pulled another cartridge out of the box. He inserted the heavy bullet, took aim, and fired.

"Another hit!" Samuelson was delighted with Slocum's accuracy with the gun. "Yesiree! You're a dead-eyed marksman!"

When the shooting was over, a total of forty-two buffalo carcasses were down in the grass. The skinners had heard the shooting and hurried out to take the hides. The two men, experts with knives, came loping through the tall grass with a rolling gait. They were followed by another man, who led a big gray mule with a special harness rig. The two skinners wore bloody buckskins, and each man carried a box of sharp knives. From a distance, Slocum saw the wagons pull out of a grove of trees and head for the killing ground.

Each skinner carried his own box of knives, Samuelson explained. Each blade was honed to a razor sharpness. The skinners had several straight ripping knives and an equal number of curved skinning blades. Skinning was hard, bloody work. The grit and dirt on the buffalo's hide quickly dulled the knives, which resulted in the blades' needing constant honing.

Slocum watched as the skinners slit the hide along the belly of the carcass from neck back to the tail. Next they cut a slash around the neck, leaving the skin on the head but keeping the ears. Then the legs were skinned with slashes along the inside.

When this was done, the skinner went back to the head and made an incision alongside each of the large, bulky ears. A rope with a metal ring was noosed and tied into these cuts.

By now the mule was backed up to the tail of the carcass. The animal was harnessed with a single tree and chain, which was hooked into the metal rings of the rope attached to the hide. When this was done, one of the skinners drove a sharp wooden stake into the buffalo's mouth. A sledgehammer was used to pound the stake deep into the prairie. This would prevent the carcass from moving when the hide was pulled off.

When these arrangements were complete, the skinner gave a command to the mule. The patient animal moved forward, and the buffalo skin was peeled neatly away from the body. Two of the teamsters rushed forward and pressed the hide into a carpetlike roll.

A man was needed at each end because the hide weighed around a hundred pounds. Once the hide was snugged and rolled, it was loaded into the wagon for the trip back to camp.

Meanwhile, Slocum and Shawnee Mike were making their way up the hillock to where their horses waited.

"You'll be good at this," Samuelson said heartily. "A man with a good eye can make plenty of money out here."

"How long will the buffalo last?" Slocum asked.

"Make your wad this season," advised the mountain man. "We're lucky to have found this bunch so close to camp. The herds aren't as big as they used to be. I figure another three or four months and the party is over. A man could follow them down into Texas, catching up with the dregs of the herd. But I don't want to fight the Kiowas and Comanches. That widow lady is waiting."

Slocum wondered about killing off the animals. "You think they'll be gone that quick?"

"Nothing but the bones will be here next spring."

"That's kind of sad."

The old man stopped at the crest of the hill. "Don't be one of those save-the-buffalo people," he said in a mild tone. "Folks talk about settling out here. Used to be there was maybe twenty million buffalo. I've seen them go past for days. Millions of animals with their hooves tearing up the prairie. Buffalo are hard on land."

"I can't dispute that," Slocum agreed.

"You can't do any farming or ranching with buffalo

around," Samuelson went on. "A few years ago I was up in Nebraska and this nester from back east built a sod house smack dab in the middle of the buffalo trail. Put it up one spring before the herd had got that far north."

"Didn't anyone warn him?" Slocum asked.

"You know how people are out here. We mind our own business."

"Did he lose the house?"

Samuelson smiled. "Lucky the herd started coming along in the morning. The nester and his family had time to run for cover. He discovered you can't treat wild animals with anything except respect. A wolverine is still a wolverine, even if you dress it up in silk pants and satin doodads. The way I look at things, we're doing the buffalo a favor by putting them out of their misery. And we're doing the country a good deed by cleaning out the herds so people can settle this land."

Slocum asked, "What about the Indians? They depend on buffalo for their food."

"Somebody always gets hurt," answered Samuelson. "That's progress."

9

Shawnee Mike Samuelson was pleased with Slocum's marksmanship. The little old man was also elated by the crew's acceptance of Slocum as a leader. After a few days had passed, Samuelson made an announcement.

"The widow woman is waiting in Kansas City," he said, sipping his second cup of thick black coffee after breakfast. "We got about five hundred hides to deliver to Dodge City. I'm going to take that Studebaker full of hides to Dodge, catch me a train to Kansas City, and spend a few days with my woman."

"Give 'er a couple punches for me," said Dallas McGhee, the head skinner.

"Slocum will be the ramrod," added Samuelson. "Anybody got problems with that?"

"Hell, no!" This came from a kid, Billy Thompson. His

voice was genial with mock gruffness. "We'll get some hides laid in. Slocum is a better shot than you."

The men laughed at the youngster's brashness, which was a way of telling the truth.

"Maybe, Mr. Wise Guy, I don't have to be a good shot," said Shawnee Mike. "I know how to hire the good ones. That counts for something."

Later, when the men had gone out to turn hides, Samuelson asked Slocum to stay in camp. The little old man poured himself another cup of coffee and added a tablespoonful of honey to the brew.

"You've done real well," he said, smiling. "Couldn't ask for a better shot. The crew is taking to you real good. What I'm wondering is if you got backbone."

"For what?"

"Not getting prodded by other men."

"Nobody ever complained."

"Good. There may be trouble when I leave. The hunting crews have run into a real hornet's nest. Several loads of hides have been hijacked."

"Why steal when buffalo are so easy to kill?" Slocum asked.

"Some people don't like work." Samuelson stirred his coffee with a tarnished spoon. "It started when a gent named Rodney Blackwell showed up in Buffalo Center. He's squeezing money from everyone. He's getting ten percent of the hide money from most hunters. That's the fee for being protected from bandits. Everyone knows Blackwell runs the bandits, but we can't prove it."

"Why hasn't someone stood up to him?"

"I did. I chased him out of camp."

"And the other hunters?"

"Maybe they don't have enough backbone. That's the polite way of putting it. They're not cowards. They're too busy making money to worry about paying off Blackwell."

"What's Rodney Blackwell got for backup?"

"A half dozen gunhands. They're real hardcases," answered Samuelson. "The worst are the Blevins brothers, a couple of rowdy ne'er-do-wells. Two-legged rattlesnake. I know they're pulling off the hide robberies, but knowing and proving are worlds apart."

"What about the law in Buffalo Center?"

Samuelson's laugh was like a coyote's bark. "Fred Derickson is the marshal. He's scared of his shadow."

Slocum wondered if Shawnee Mike Samuelson was turning tail. A showdown could be coming, and Kansas City would be a safe haven if bullets started flying. "You think Blackwell's bunch will make trouble?" he asked.

"They might when they hear I'm gone. They'll probably come out and test your mettle."

"I don't enjoy another man's fight," Slocum said. "I hired on as a shooter. That means I kill buffalo, not men."

A sharp expression appeared on Samuelson's face. "I'm not asking you to be a gunfighter. Just stand up for me and the crew while I'm gone."

"Nobody pushes me," Slocum replied.

"Good. I wanted you to be aware of Blackwell's snakes." Samuelson poured the dregs of his coffee out on the ground. He set the cup on the tailgate of the chuck wagon. "You're in charge, Slocum. I'll stop in Buffalo Center and tell the butcher to get his meat from someone else."

Before Samuelson left camp he gave Slocum a thick roll of greenbacks for payroll and expenses. Then the little old man hooked up his mules, got on the seat of the Studebaker wagon, and rolled out of camp toward the trail to Dodge City.

The days that followed were filled with hard work. Every man in the group, including John Slocum, put in long, tiresome hours. Shooting and skinning a buffalo was just the beginning of a long process that led to a cured hide. After hides were skinned and brought to camp, they were taken off the wagon and laid on the ground, flesh side up.

Then the skinners slashed small holes all around the hide. Two dozen wooden pegs were driven through these slits and into the earth. The pegs were cut from willow or other tree limbs.

When the hide was stretched out, it was "poisoned" against insects and vermin. This involved a heavy drenching with water laced with arsenic. Unless the poison was spread over the hide, hide bugs and worms ate holes throughout the surface.

Another problem was that the dead vermin appealed to birds. Bluejays, ravens, and magpies ate the poisoned worms and bugs, then sickened and died. Every evening the crew had to go out an clear away the dead birds that littered the ground around the hides.

Three days in the Kansas sun would set a hide as stiff as a pine board. Then the pegs had to be pulled out and the hide reversed to dry the hair side. After another two or three days of drying, the hides were pulled up and stacked in piles about one hundred high.

These stacks of hides still needed to be cured. It took one man most of the morning to spread the hides over the prairie to cure in the sun until noon. Then the hides were turned so the opposite side could cure in the afternoon. Hides had to be stacked each evening. Otherwise, the dewdrops would cause the hide to curl up along the edges.

Once the sun had burned the moisture out of a hide, it was about half the original weight. Those that were cured were known as flint hides. The hide from a buffalo cow ended up weighing about forty pounds, while a bull's hide would be forty-five to fifty pounds.

The hide of a young bull was light, thin, and weighed about twenty-five pounds. When the cure was completed, the hides were rolled up and stored on a wagon under a protective canvas tarp. Hunters and hiders worked from daylight to dark and always seemed to be behind schedule.

* * *

The day after Samuelson left, the crew was eating their noon meal in camp. Slocum saw three riders coming from the direction of Buffalo Center. They rode as if they owned the land and everything on it. They spurred their horses, charging up the hillock. The lead rider was a lanky man with a hatchet face. He had a hard, insolent manner. The other two men were tall and bulky, and their features were scarred and battered. The youngest one was a fair-haired man about thirty wearing a black-and-white cowhide vest. They wore gunbelts with tied-down holsters.

They didn't stop to ask if they were welcome in camp. They swung down out of their saddles and swaggered over to where the crew was gathered by the chuck wagon. Spur chains jangled as their booted feet pounded against the earth.

The lanky man paused for a moment, sizing up the men gathered for the noon meal. Then he curled his lip and walked forward. "We're looking for the head man," he said.

Slocum looked up with a faint grin. "That would be me."

"You made a bad mistake taking over for Samuelson," said the hardcase. He kept his hand away from his holstered gun. "Folks around here don't like saddle tramps moving in. We're going to make you sorry you ever shot a buffalo. Bucko, you're going to remember me."

Slocum had set his plate aside, stood up, and readied himself for the man's move. The other men in the crew fell back as the lanky man swung at Slocum's head. The shiny metal of steel knuckles glinted in the sunlight.

Slocum jerked his head back, and the steeled fist went whistling past. Then, with the lanky man off balance, Slocum slammed his fist into the man's Adam's apple. The man made a strangled sound and clawed at his throat.

Slocum stepped forward and smashed a powerful blow

into the croaking man's stomach. All the air went out of the man's lungs with a whooshing noise. He fell forward on the ground like a rag doll, gasping for breath.

The two bulky men looked down at their fallen friend.

"Lordy," said the man in the cowhide vest.

"Get him out of here!" Slocum commanded.

"I just might try you on for size, mister." The vested man's hand started to move toward his holstered pistol.

John Slocum eased into a crouch. His voice turned taut and flat in tone. "Don't try it."

The man in the vest made the motions of a man who was beaten. It was an old gunman's trick, and Slocum wasn't buying the ruse. He kept his gaze fixed on the gunman's hand.

The man was turning away from Slocum when his draw started.

Slocum moved in a quick, fluid motion. His pistol cleared leather like coiled lightning. He snapped the gun up and pulled back the hammer.

The hardcase spun around, still trying to get his gun out of the holster. His face took on an ashen pall, his dark eyes almost rolled up into their sockets. His mouth dropped open, and spittle drooled out onto his chin.

The camp became deathly quiet.

Then a slow, bubbling sound began down in the man's throat. His rawboned body seemed to shrink. He made a moaning noise that was thick and liquid. His body seemed to hang motionless under the muzzle of Slocum's revolver.

The third man had a surprised, horrified look. Slowly he raised his hands high above his head.

Slocum holstered his pistol as quickly as the weapon had been drawn. "Get going," he said.

"Thank you," gurgled the man in the vest. "Thank you, sir."

Slocum jerked his thumb toward the lanky man, who was rolling on the ground. "Take your trash with you."

Instead the vested man ran to his horse and leaped up

into the saddle. He spurred his animal into a fast gallop.
The crew moved forward and grabbed the lanky man by
the back of his shirt. Dallas McGhee, the skinner, laid the
man across his saddle and slapped the flanks of his horse.
The animal took off down the slope.

The third man was already mounted and riding out of
camp. Like the man in the vest, he didn't look back.

"Lordy! I never seen anybody draw a gun like that,"
said McGhee.

"Yeah, that was something," said Billy Thompson.

Slocum shrugged. "Let's finish eating and get back to
work. If we get done early I'll spring for a visit to the
cathouse in town."

"Chasing off those yahoos is worth celebrating," agreed
Dallas McGhee. "Let's get moving, boys, and get the hides
in."

After supper, the cook volunteered to stay in camp as a
guard. Slocum led his crew of hiders into Buffalo Center.
The saloons and gambling halls were filled with men
searching for liquor and excitement. Buffalo Center
seemed to be a sleepy town during the day, but it came to
life after the sun went down.

The brothel was located on the southern edge of the
business area. The establishment was identified by a red
china lamp burning in the window. Slocum and his men
tied their horses to a hitching post in front of the two-stor-
ied house.

They walked up on the porch and were greeted by a
middle-aged woman in a thin robe.

"Welcome boys." She opened the door and stepped out
on the porch. "I'm Madam Sophie. You came to the right
place if you're looking for fun and women."

"That sounds good," Slocum said.

"Two dollars a head," said Madam Sophie. "I guarantee
you gents will be satisfied. You won't find any virgins, but
I've got attractive women to pick from."

"My treat," said Slocum. He peeled some greenbacks off his wad and handed them to the madam.

"Go inside and take your pick, gents," said Sophie, tucking the bills into the pocket of her robe. "This ain't the house of all nations, but our prices are right."

The parlor was furnished with two horsehair sofas, a small end table, and two lamps. A thick carpet was rolled up along the wall.

"I wanted a nicer place," Sophie said, "but the buffalo men kept bringing in fleas. Between the boots, the bull crap, and bugs I decided to keep a bare floor."

Slocum and his men settled down on the sofas. Madam Sophie clapped her hands, and several attractive women walked down the stairs. They wore cotton robes opened to reveal their attributes.

"They're paid for, girls," the madam said, "so be sure and show these customers a good time."

"I'm Beulah," said a buxom young woman with ample breasts. She walked around the parlor, and her breast jiggled with each step.

The second woman down the stairway was a tall blond with a slender, boyish build. "Folks call me Misty," she announced in a sexy voice.

The third was a short, black-haired girl with plenty of pounds. "Laurie is my name," she said. "I'm game for any man who likes fat girls."

"Red's my name," said a redheaded woman, "and bed's my game."

A brown-haired girl with an attractive figure joined the group. "My name is Lil," she purred, "and I'm known to give my customers a thrill."

Madam Sophie spoke up. "You gents getting any ideas?"

"Hell, we're enjoying looking over the herd," Slocum said.

Everyone laughed.

Madam Sophie giggled as she walked over to the bottom of the stairway.

"Now, gents, you're going to feast your eyes on someone special. This is no two-dollar whore. She goes for twenty dollars, and Annie is as close to a virgin as you'll ever find in a cathouse. Annie is young, but she's been taught by her sisters how to please a man. Now, feast your eyes on Annie—the star of the house."

A blond girl with long golden curls, a finely featured face, and a delicate, small-boned body stepped into view. She wore a white chemise and walked with a fluid, easy motion.

"God, she's beautiful!!" whispered young Billy Thompson. "She must be about my age."

"What's that?" asked Slocum.

"I'm eighteen, best as I know," Billy replied. He kept staring at the girl called Annie, who had kept her chemise buttoned.

"Annie's a bit shy," explained Madam Sophie. "Aren't you, chile?"

"Yes, ma'am." The girl's diction was refined.

Slocum knew Annie was not a child of the frontier. "Where you from, honey?" he asked.

"Indiana," Annie replied, blushing.

"Her folks were headed west in a covered wagon," Madam Sophie said. "They got attacked by Comanches. Her parents were killed, and Annie is an orphan. I took the poor chile in because she's so beautiful. Pretty as a picture."

Annie blushed. "Now, Mother Sophie—" she began.

"Truth never hurt anyone," said the madam. "You're like a living doll. Gentlemen, the girls and I have grown fond of Annie. We don't allow her to drink whiskey or take drugs. I'm not going to wear her out on two-dollar customers, so Annie's price is twenty bucks. And she doesn't get showed to the ugly, brutal buffalo men who wouldn't treasure her. Now, what's your choice?"

Dallas McGhee, the boss skinner, picked the first woman, the one with the animated breasts. "I got to find out if those things are real, Beulah."

"Well, let's go upstairs and you'll find out." The woman took the skinner's hand and headed up the stairs.

The other skinners took the women standing closest to them and started up the stairs.

"Those men know what life is about," commented Sophie. "They know women are about the same in bed. Now, young man, what's your pick?"

Billy Thompson looked down at his shoes. "If you don't mind, ma'am, I'd . . . well, you see . . ."

"We deal in all sorts of services, son," the madam said. "Just let me know your desires. You want to get spanked? Locked up in handcuffs and beaten with a belt? A golden shower? Those things cost extra, of course, but we want our customers satisfied."

Slocum looked at the young man. "What'll it be, Billy?"

"You won't laugh?"

"Nope."

"I'd like to stay down here and talk to Annie."

"An admirable choice," said Sophie cheerfully. She took the two young people by the hand and led them out into the kitchen. "Talk as long as you want."

"Well, Lil, that leaves you and me," Slocum said.

She smiled. "Disappointed? If you are, I can call more girls from upstairs."

"You look just right for me," Slocum said.

"I'm a good lay. I take pride in my work." She walked over and took Slocum's hand, and they went upstairs.

Her room was at the end of the upstairs hall. "You fellows new in town?" she asked, opening the door.

"I'm new."

"Sit down on the bed," Lil said. "I'll take off your boots."

Slocum relaxed as Lil busied herself with his clothing,

removing his boots, pulling his shirt off, and running her hands over his chest. He nibbled the nipples of her finely formed breasts, which were taut and firm.

He abandoned her breasts and undressed completely, laying his gunbelt on the bedside table. As he joined her on the bed, she reached for the rigid column of flesh between his legs. She stroked it with a long, gentle movement.

"God, there isn't anything I like better than a good hard cock," she said.

Then she kissed him on the lips. He could tell by the quiver of her body that she was ready.

She rolled over on her back, spread her legs, and Slocum pressed against the warm wetness. Then he was inside her, feeling the warm velvety smoothness of her tunnel.

She wrapped her powerful legs around him. He moved in and out of her while she eagerly kissed his neck, face, and mouth. He could feel her reaching a plateau. That was when she thrust her tongue deep into his mouth, humming and moaning so that his teeth vibrated. He sucked her tongue with all of his strength. It seemed that while he was making love to her with his penis, she was doing the same to him with her tongue.

Locked inside her powerful thighs, Slocum tried to hold back to enjoy more time with her. But Lil seemed to anticipate his intentions. She pulled her mouth loose and started moaning aloud. Then she started a grinding pelvic motion that met his thrusts, twirled around them, and pulled him deeper inside her.

She moaned with pleasure when he erupted inside her. Her eyes were closed, and a pleased smile tugged the corners of her lips. Her insides milked him of every drop of seed.

"Mister, I oughta pay *you*," she purred in a husky voice.

"I won't resist."

She smiled up at him. "Ever think of opening your own tomcat house for women?"

"I wouldn't last very long."

"The housewives and the matrons would go wild," Lil said. "Come on, get up now and I'll help put your clothes on. Now, where do you fellows camp?"

"Out on the prairie."

"Don't get smart, mister. What's your name?"

"John Slocum."

"Well, I thought it might be nice to ride out to your camp tomorrow."

"You'd certainly be welcome."

"That Billy work with you?"

"He's one of the crew."

"Good." Lil smiled. "I think him and Annie should get better acquainted. Is he a nice person?"

"He's a good worker."

"Would he make a good husband?" she asked.

"Oh-hoo! Now I know what you're after." Slocum was dressed now. He stood there, letting his hand glide over the silken smoothness of her skin.

"Well, Annie isn't really a whore," Lil explained. "Sophie makes her get dressed up and parade around. But our hard-hearted madam would die if someone tried to bed down Miss Annie. But if she lives in a place like this long enough, she's going to start working. I don't want her to become a chippie. The girl's had good upbringing, Slocum."

"Come out for lunch tomorrow," suggested Slocum. "The cook is better than most. I'll tell him ladies are coming. He'll kill himself fixing things for you."

"That's us." Lil placed a kiss on his cheek. "Just a couple of secret matchmakers."

"Maybe Billy doesn't want to get married."

Still nude, she looked up at him with a serious expression. "I know men better than you do, Slocum. A kid is in love if he wants to talk instead of screw. Most of them are so hot they'll come in their pants watching a girl undress. Then they beg you not to tell their friends. Nope, Billy gave up a good lay tonight to talk with Annie. He's head over heels in love."

"Poor Billy! You girls will have him hog-tied and up to the altar in a week."

Lil turned and looked at Slocum with a smile. "Slocum, we're fast workers. We don't need a week. See you tomorrow, honey."

Slocum collected his men and they sang a rowdy song, "Roll Me Over in the Clover," on the trail back to camp.

10

Rodney Blackwell's skull-like face was unnaturally pale for someone living on the frontier. This was because he seldom ventured out into the sunlight. Thirty-eight years old, Blackwell was a creature of saloons and frontier night life. He enjoyed staying up until the last drink was poured.

Blackwell's Crystal Palace was the largest saloon in Buffalo Center. The drinking spot was a hangout for hard-cases from all over the frontier. The saloon featured a horseshoe bar, scores of tables, a stage for dancing girls, and musicians. The saloon was crowded every night with hunters and hiders in from the plains.

Blackwell's office was in the back of the Crystal Palace. It was furnished with a brand-new roll-top desk, several decrepit chairs, and two large brass spitoons. The office served as the collecting place for the money paid by the brothels, gambling dens, saloons, buffalo hunters and hiders, and the merchants in town.

Blackwell's men made weekly collections from the local business firms. The merchants knew their protective payments kept Blackwell's gang at bay. In addition, people who opposed Blackwell often died from lead poisoning.

Everyone remembered the old man who set up a freight service hauling supplies from Dodge City. When Blackwell's men came around for their collection, the old man laughed. He said the United States was a free country, by god, and he wasn't paying extortion money to any tinhorn tyrants. A week later the old man was bushwhacked on a trip back from Dodge City.

After that killing, some merchants added a little extra to their weekly payments to get Blackwell's goodwill. Paying protection money was part of the cost of doing business in Buffalo Center. No one wanted to tangle with Blackwell's hardcases for a measly ten percent of their income.

Rodney Blackwell had gained the catbird's seat by hiring the toughest hoodlums on the frontier. Seventeen gunmen were on his payroll. A sizable number of drifters worked by the job, taking their pay in whiskey and food. They were all hard hombres—although it rankled Blackwell that three of his men had turned tail out at Samuelson's camp.

Now, sitting in his office, Blackwell's mind was fogged by a lingering hangover from the previous night's drinking. His bilious stomach was also the result of overindulgence. He decided to quit drinking to be sure alcohol wasn't becoming a habit.

Whenever he was hung over, Rodney Blackwell remembered his last drunk in Indiana. He had killed a whore during a drunken fight over her money. He woke up in jail with a lynch mob forming in the town square. Rather than see a man hung without trial, the jailer opened the cell and let Blackwell escape. He had fled west, settling first in Missouri and later drifting to western Kansas.

Blackwell had wanted to nurse his hangover alone in his office, but the bartender had shown in a hardcase up from Texas. The stranger was a rough-featured man who wore a Colt Dragoon tied down in a cowhide holster. He looked like a man down on his luck.

The stranger said he was looking for work.

"Plenty to do for able-bodied men around here," said Blackwell. He was too cagey to discuss anything openly with a stranger. "You might try the livery stable or hook up with one of the buffalo crews."

"I don't mean that kind of work," said the stranger. "I'm Manny Fargo."

An expression of surprise came over Blackwell's face. "I heard you were dead. Something about a shoot-out down in El Paso."

Manny Fargo shook his head negatively. "There was a hellish amount of lead flying my way, but I managed to get out without any extra weight."

Blackwell was interested in hiring the stranger. "Everyone knows you're one of the fastest men in the West. I'll bet you didn't do it with that pistol."

"Hell, no," said Fargo, smiling. "That El Paso shoot-out started over a gal I was sleeping with. Her husband took a notion he didn't like it. I was about half drunk in the saloon. It was a nice place. Everybody checked their gunbelts at the door. I went out the back door when the husband and his friends came charging in. Not a gun on me, and a half-dozen Mexicans after my tail. I come out of the alley and saw this old-timer wearing this Dragoon model. I grabbed it and shot the husband and two of his friends. Then I hightailed it up here. The boys out in front said you was hiring gunhands."

"Just the best," said Blackwell.

Fargo sneered. "That isn't what the talk is in town. I hear a couple of your boys got taken down a peg yesterday. Some buffalo hunter cleaned their clock. People are saying all three men are still running."

"They were amateurs," snapped Blackwell.

"That's why I come to see you."

"You figuring on doing better?"

Manny Fargo pushed back his sombrero. "Mister, I'm forty years old. I've killed thirteen men. Nobody bones me. I ride my own pace."

"There's even a song out about you." Blackwell liked gunmen who had a reputation. "But how do I know you're really Manny Fargo? Maybe you just made up the story to get a job."

Fargo gave Blackwell a stony look.

"Just asking," Blackwell said.

"Watch this." Manny Fargo raised his right hand above his shoulder. "Say when."

"Now."

Rodney Blackwell's lips were still closing when he looked into the muzzle of the Colt Dragoon.

"I don't mess around," snapped Fargo. He shoved the pistol back into his holster. "You looking for a good hand, or are you just blowing smoke?"

"I'm interested."

"A hundred a month and grub buys me."

"Manny Fargo, you're hired!" Rodney Blackwell was so happy he forgot to haggle over the price. "Take a seat and I'll let you in on what things are about around here."

Fargo dropped down into a scarred chair. "I hear you've got things sewed tight here."

"That's why I need you. I aim to keep things that way."

"You run a protection racket?"

"Nicest you'll ever hear of," bragged Blackwell. "See, when I got out here there wasn't anything but prairie. Any fool could see the buffalo hunters needed something to do. Saloons, stores, everything you can get in Dodge City, Abilene, or even Kansas City. So I started the Crystal Palace, and other folks started moving in. Pretty soon we had a couple people wanting to start stores. See, I started everything, so I deserve being paid. Right?"

"I don't care whether you're right or wrong," answered Fargo. "You just pay me."

"Thing is, some people are starting to hold out. This old mountain man used to flap his jaws a lot. He didn't pay me. You ever hear of him? Shawnee Mike Samuelson's his name."

Fargo nodded. "His camp where the trouble took place yesterday?"

Blackwell nodded.

"You want me to roust him?"

Blackwell spread his hands. "It wasn't Samuelson who did it, but some new guy named John Slocum."

Manny Fargo stiffened.

"You know him?" asked Blackwell.

"He's good."

"Three of my boys are scared of him."

"You want me to get Slocum?"

Blackwell made a steeple with his fingers. He considered the possibility. "No, it might draw attention from the U.S. marshal. A little extorting, a little hijacking and nobody cares. Too many murders and people get nosy."

Fargo wasn't concerned about a U.S. marshal. "I could do it so he just disappears."

"I'll let you know."

"What about this Shawnee Mike?" asked Fargo.

"A couple of Indians"—Blackwell winked—"got him last night. I heard there were a lot of hides on his wagon."

"Real Indians?" asked Fargo.

"Who knows?" Blackwell's hangover was getting better, and he wanted to show off his new gunman. "Let's go out and meet some of the local folks."

The morning was as bright as brass, and the sky was cloudless. A light breeze, thick with the smell of dead animals, blew into camp. Huge flocks of butterflies fluttered in the grass. High above the camp a pair of black hawks circled in the sky.

After their night in town, the crew of hiders worked with a relaxed attitude. After shooting his day's quota of buffalo, John Slocum saddled up his horse and rode into Buffalo Center. He was running low on cartridges for the big Sharps .50-caliber buffalo gun. His first stop was at the gunsmith's shop, where he picked up 250 rounds of the special ammunition. That would last for a week, Slocum figured.

The gunsmith was a genial man who made a good living fixing guns and loading cartridges for the hunters. He left his shop and walked out to the hitching post with Slocum. "You hear about the Indians?" he asked.

Slocum asked, "What happened?"

"They killed a man last night," said the gunsmith. "Shawnee Mike Samuelson. You know him? A little wiry fellow who likes Studebaker wagons."

Shawnee Mike dead? Slocum could not believe the news. "Who told you?" he asked.

"Matt Johnson. He's the undertaker. He went out and brought in the body."

"You know how Samuelson was killed?"

"Just Indians, I guess," the gunsmith replied. "The body's over at Matt Johnson's place. He's getting it ready for the funeral."

"Where's that?" Slocum asked.

"In back of Johnson's harness shop. Down in the next block."

"Thanks." Slocum got up into the saddle.

"Do you know him?" asked the gunsmith. "Was he a friend of yours?"

Slocum spurred his horse and left the gunsmith standing by the hitching rail.

Matt Johnson was a short, energetic man in his mid-forties. He had settled in Buffalo Center to make harness. When a skinner was killed by a rampaging buffalo bull, Johnson offered to make a pinewood coffin. From that beginning,

Johnson became the man to call in town when a burial was needed.

Johnson was in a back room behind his shop with two other men. They were hammering together a pine box coffin.

The harness maker looked up when Slocum appeared in the doorway. "Help you?"

"I heard Shawnee Mike Samuelson got killed," said Slocum.

"Yep. Indians got him last night or early this morning. The body's back here. I wrapped him in canvas to bring him in. We're planning on burying him in a couple of hours. We don't have any way to keep a body. They start stinking after a few hours in this heat."

"Could I see him?"

"Sure. I reckon he won't mind." Johnson gestured toward a table near the door. "A friend of yours?"

"I worked for him."

Johnson nodded. "You must be the new man folks are talking about. You got some ginger in you, I reckon. Nobody ever takes on Blackwell's bunch. You and Mike are the only ones."

Slocum walked over and opened up the canvas covering the body. Shawnee Mike Samuelson's bloody face looked up at the man from Georgia.

"Those red devils must've pounded his head a dozen times. The tomahawk is out in the wagon." Johnson paused and looked down at Shawnee Mike's head. "Somebody ought to clean out the whole kit and caboodle for killing a man like that."

"Where'd they get him?"

"A campground between here and Dodge City."

"Poor Mike." Slocum laid the canvas back over the body. "What time is the funeral going to be held?"

"Me and the boys ought to get the box nailed together by two o'clock. Then we got to go around and tell everybody what time we'll be putting him away. I'd say three o'clock."

"What did you do with his wagon and the hides?" Slocum asked.

Matt Johnson looked confused. "There wasn't a wagon or hides anywhere near the body. Just the body lying out there by the river."

"You notify the sheriff?"

"Deputy sheriff come out from the county seat. He left about thirty minutes ago."

Slocum said, "Don't hold the funeral until I get back with his crew. They'll want to be present."

"We got Ike Peabody to read over the body," said Johnson. "He's a real good preacher. Drinks too much, but his words are pretty if he's sober."

Slocum led the hiders into Buffalo Center for the funeral. No one in town had thought to build a church, so the services for Shawnee Mike would be at the graveyard—a vacant lot on the edge of town containing a half-dozen graves marked with white pine crosses.

About fifty people gathered around the grave. Among them were Lil and Annie, Madam Sophie, Homer Hotchkiss, and the livery stable owner, George Lewis. Lewis was accompanied by a tired-looking woman who held a baby on her hip and smoked a corncob pipe. Lewis and his wife were surrounded by a scattering of kids, all of whom talked in a loud, irritating manner.

Homer Hotchkiss walked over and whispered to Slocum, "I see Rodney Blackwell and his thugs are absent."

Slocum's tone was bitter. "They're probably selling the hides."

Hotchkiss nudged Slocum's arm. "Here comes the preacher. He looks downright soused. Chrissakes, Ike Peabody is going to die a drunkard's death."

A red-faced man in a black suit, white shirt, and black string tie staggered through the crowd. He carried a Bible in his hands. "Are any of the deceased relatives here?" Ike Peabody wanted to know. He waited a moment for someone to step forward.

"He ain't got no relatives I know of," said Dallas McGhee. "Mike was always too busy in the wilderness."

"I always like to ask," said Peabody. He started to open his Bible, staggered, and almost fell in the grave.

"Watch him, boys!" cried Madam Sophie.

"Careful, Ike," snapped Matt Johnson.

"Don't tell me how to read over a body," snapped the preacher. "I done it before."

"Get started," said Hotchkiss. "This sun isn't getting any cooler."

"You want to do it?" said Peabody in a peevish tone.

"Go ahead," answered the doctor.

"Listen up, you people. This here is a pine box holding the remains of Shawnee Mike Samuelson," said Peabody. "Take him, Lord, and may those red Indians drop dead before nightfall. Amen! Awright, shove him in, boys."

"Darn good service," said Madam Sophie.

11

Homer Hotchkiss walked with Slocum as the crowd left the graveyard and started back to town.

"A tragedy," said Hotchkiss. "I didn't know Samuelson, but he deserved a better end. The burying crew said the Indians had chopped him up pretty bad."

"It wasn't Indians, Doc," Slocum said. "Mike's hides and his Studebaker wagon are gone."

"Indians have been known to steal."

"I never knew a tribe to go after buffalo hides," Slocum said.

"Maybe they thought there was whiskey in the wagon."

"That's possible," Slocum agreed. "But you and I know who killed Samuelson. The murder was done by Rodney Blackwell and his gang of thieves. Shawnee Mike wasn't paying protection money to Blackwell's gang. His wagon was an open target for hijacking."

"Blackwell's just a two-bit saloon owner," Hotchkiss said.

"You've met him?"

"I've had a couple of drinks at the Crystal Palace. The name doesn't fit the place."

They came to the main street of Buffalo Center. The Crystal Palace was on the corner of the next block.

"We ought to clean out that nest of hoodlums," Slocum said. "Do you think these people will back me up?"

Hotchkiss snorted. "Not likely. They don't have backbones."

"Well, at least the hiders will back me up."

"I wouldn't be too sure," Hotchkiss said. "Shawnee Mike was undoubtedly a likable man. But he's dead, and your hiders have to think about surviving."

Slocum stopped walking into town. He waited until the crew of hiders came walking up.

"A short service," said Dallas McGhee. "Just as well. Mike wouldn't like a big show."

The other men gathered around Slocum and the skinner.

"I'm going after Blackwell," Slocum said. "I figure his bunch did Mike in for the wagonload of hides. They're a mean bunch, and I'm going to need backing up."

The men looked down at the ground.

"I'm not much for gunplay," Dallas McGhee said.

"Me neither," said Billy Thompson. "Besides, I'm going over to talk to Annie. I think she wants to get married."

Slocum looked at the rest of the men.

They turned their heads and looked away. Heads down, they left Slocum standing in the afternoon sun.

"See you out to the camp," McGhee said.

Homer Hotchkiss stood and watched the crew walk toward the livery stables to get their animals. "I told you they would be like that. People don't hurry into a fight."

"I'll go it alone," Slocum said. "Shawnee Mike deserves some justice for the way he was killed."

"I saw the tomahawk," Hotchkiss said. "Pure Indian."

Slocum asked, "Why don't you come with me?"

Hotchkiss held up his hand, palm outward. "No way I'm going to get involved. Buffalo Center is just another bend in the road for me. I'm not getting mixed up in gunplay."

As Slocum walked toward the Crystal Palace, Rodney Blackwell stood at the end of the bar in the saloon. The Crystal Palace had a half-dozen patrons, three ladies who were called dancers, and the Blackwell gang.

Manny Fargo was standing beside Blackwell and swelling up with self-importance. The Texas gunfighter was a big man, rawboned and tall. His face was marked with high cheekbones, and a knife scar on his forehead, and a nose with a broken and poorly set bridge. He had broad shoulders and a lean, narrow-waisted body.

Fargo was drinking his third shot of whiskey and enjoying admiring glances from Blackwell's gang. He stood with his back to the wall of the Crystal Palace, not allowing anyone to stand behind him.

Fargo knew that his reputation had been swelled up by the publication of a dime novel in the East. The book, *The Prince of the Pistols,* had been written by a hack writer who had never been west of the Hudson River. The book told of Fargo's defense of pretty young women, his love for his mother, and his gallantry in battle.

Fargo had signed a contract and received $300 from the publishing company. The only pretty girls Fargo had met he'd tried to rape. His mother was a saloon girl who had died of cirrhosis of the liver. And Fargo's gallantry included shooting his enemies in the back. That way you didn't have to look into the muzzles of their pistols.

Fargo was fast with a gun. After the book came out,

he'd taken time to perfect his fast draw. Although he liked the $300 payment from the publisher, the book caused trouble for him. It seemed like every punk in the West wanted to be known as the man who killed Manny Fargo.

So the gunman from Texas kept his back to the wall, watched the hands of the people around him, and didn't get too drunk. These precautions allowed him to stay alive and profit from his reputation. Men like Rodney Blackwell paid well for a good hand with a gun.

Fargo went easy on his drink. The whiskey in the Crystal Palace was snakehead rotgut that would eat the lining out of a man's stomach. But something told him to stay alert, that trouble was brewing in Buffalo Center. Manny wanted to be about three seconds ahead of the other man when lead started flying.

Fargo expected to tangle with John Slocum if he stayed on the Blackwell payroll. The notion didn't appeal to the Texan because he'd seen Slocum in action. Slocum was a powder keg with a short fuse, and he could fight like an Apache on a drunken rampage.

Fargo had seen Slocum take two men out in an argument in a little town in east Texas. Slocum was a quiet man with green eyes that never blinked. A gambler had tried to deal from the bottom of the deck. Slocum nailed the tinhorn, then pistol-whipped the two local toughs who tried to pull their guns.

Right now, Manny Fargo was also wondering about Rodney Blackwell. His new boss didn't even carry a gun, not even a hideaway derringer. That seemed downright stupid to a man like Manny Fargo. And stupid was how Fargo sized up Rodney Blackwell. The man was like the hardcases in his gang—easily impressed by Fargo's reputation.

Most of the Blackwell gang were frontier badmen, mostly young punks who would knife, club, or shoot a man for whatever was in his pocket. A couple of them looked as if they might stay around to celebrate their thirtieth birthday. These men were on the prod, looking for a quick reputation. Manny Fargo's dead body was a ticket to that claim to glory.

There was also a sprinkling of middle-aged gunhands on the payroll. These men were real rattlesnakes. They'd been smart enough to survive over the years without catching lead poisoning. When the bullets started flying, Manny figured, the older gunhands stayed a good mile away.

Rodney Blackwell nudged Manny Fargo with his elbow. "I think trouble just walked through the door." Blackwell pointed to the tall man in buckskins who had walked into the Crystal Palace. "I'll bet that's John Slocum."

Manny Fargo saw the lean, knife-blade body and knew it was Slocum. He liked the way Slocum paused after coming through the swinging doors, those green eyes scanning the room and sizing up everyone.

Manny watched as a tired saloon girl rushed up to Slocum's side. "Come on in," the woman said with a smile. "You must be new in town. I'm Rose."

"Some other time," Slocum said.

Rose looked offended. "I was just trying to be sociable."

"I'm looking for Rodney Blackwell," Slocum told her.

"He's back at the end of the bar," Rose said. "He's the one in the black suit."

Slocum walked further into the Crystal Palace. His gaze swept over the gunmen who were lounging at tables or bellied up against the bar. They were sorry-looking specimens of humanity, Slocum decided. He could feel the tension in the saloon—a thick atmosphere of hatred, fear, and greed.

Carefully, walking like a cat on the balls of his feet, Slocum walked to the back of the Crystal Palace.

Rodney Blackwell stood at the bar. His hands were open and in full view. A nervous tic twisted the edge of Blackwell's mouth. His mouth opened, and his green-coated tongue wetted his lips.

Slocum walked a couple of steps past Blackwell and then turned around to have a full view of the saloon.

"The lady said you're Blackwell." Slocum's tone was as hard as sunbaked adobe bricks.

"At your service," Rodney answered with a quick smile. "I figure you're John Slocum."

"You figured right."

"Sorry to hear about Shawnee Mike's Death," Blackwell said. "He and I had our differences, no doubt about that. But he seemed like a good man."

"He was one of the best."

"Good friends are hard to find." The tic on Blackwell's face pumped faster.

"Any idea who might have done it?"

Blackwell's face was stony. "I heard it was Indians."

"A wagonload of hides are missing."

"Sorry to hear that, Slocum." Blackwell turned around carefully, keeping his hands in full view. "I'm a peaceful man. I'm in the insurance business. Shawnee Mike didn't want to buy a policy. I don't insure against Indian attacks, so my policy wouldn't have helped him."

"Mike said you were running a protection racket."

"People have different outlooks on business," said Blackwell. His hands came up, and his thin, bony fingers snapped. "How awkward of me. I'm not being a good host. Let me buy you a drink."

"No thanks. I don't feel welcome here." Slocum's gaze swept across the gunmen.

"They're salesmen," said Blackwell. He slapped his hand against the mahogany bar. "Give the man a shot of our best whiskey. Pour a couple of fingers from the premium bottle."

"I don't want it."

"Relax, Slocum. You're among friends." Blackwell's

smile was quick, phony. He raised his voice and addressed the people in the saloon. "Folks, this is a new acquaintance of mine, John Slocum. Nothing to worry about. Go on with your talking and cardplaying."

Slocum looked at Blackwell with a hard stare. "I figured your boys might have done in Shawnee Mike."

"We're not murderers, sir!" Blackwell sounded offended. "But I'll forgo your insinuation. I've been discussing the future with my new sales manager. We're looking for another hand. I think you could fit the bill, Slocum. The position pays a hundred dollars a month."

"And found," spoke up Manny Fargo.

Slocum said, "He's your new man?"

"Yep."

Slocum studied Fargo's face for an instant. He furrowed his brow for a moment, then said, "A little town in east Texas. A couple of years back. You were drinking with a saloon lady."

Fargo was impressed. "I'm Manny Fargo. You got a good memory, mister."

Slocum studied the gunfighter for a few seconds. "When did you get into town?"

"This morning."

"You come from Dodge City?"

Fargo shook his head. "I rode in from Texas, Slocum. Don't try to pin the murder on me. Are you the law in this burg?"

"I'm just checking into Mike's death."

"Don't start sniffing around me," said Fargo. His voice was low, menacing. "I don't like busybodies poking around."

Blackwell glared at Fargo. "Slocum didn't mean anything by it."

"I don't like a man to prod me," snapped Fargo. "I saw you in action, Slocum. Folks say you're a Georgia man. A sharpshooter and a real fast draw. Supposed to have run with Quantrill's bunch during the war."

"You're mostly right."

"Your luck has been running pretty good," Fargo went on. "You're supposed to have a charmed life getting in and out of scrapes."

"I've heard that tale."

"Don't press your luck," Fargo went on. "Every man's string runs out one time or another."

"I'd say that was good advice for any man," Slocum said to the Texan.

The bartender set up with fresh drinks for Blackwell and Fargo. He wiped the top of the bar, set down a coaster, and placed a double shot glass of whiskey in front of Slocum.

"To your health." Blackwell smiled, but his eyes were mirthless.

"To a long life, Slocum." Manny Fargo raised his glass to a toasting position.

Slocum stared at Blackwell. "If your boys didn't kill Shawnee Mike, who did?"

"Indians," answered Blackwell. "Just like everyone says."

A man at a nearby table giggled. His laugh was nervous, tense. Blackwell gave the man a cold stare.

Slocum looked around the saloon. "I see you've got three men missing. Where are the so-called salesmen you sent out to my camp yesterday?"

"They left town," said Blackwell.

"Like you'll do if you're smart," added Fargo.

"He can work for us," Blackwell went on. "The pay is generous, Slocum, and this town has a great future. The buffalo herds will soon be gone. This is probably the last good year. But the Atchison, Topeka and Santa Fe railroad has a plan to bring in homesteaders. Buffalo Center can be the biggest town in this part of the state. Throw in with me. We're not murderers but honest businessmen. I started this town from scratch when it was nothing but a piece of sod out on the prairie."

Slocum looked surprised. "You set up Buffalo Center?"

"Didn't do a very good job of it." Blackwell laughed. "The next time I start up a town I'll have some experience. Anyway, the money will roll in when the homesteaders come out here. They're family men, Slocum. Nesters, that's what cowboys call them. You could be a congressman. Maybe even governor. I got plans to back some men in politics. You got all kinds of chances to make money in politics. Hell, maybe you could even be elected to the Senate. How does 'Senator Slocum' sound?"

"Forget the pipe dreams."

"Just showing what the future can be." Blackwell shrugged. "This is new country, Slocum. But the frontier is changing. The days are slim and few for men who drift around from town to town. The days of carrying guns will soon be over. A man has to look to the future."

"No thanks," Slocum said. He pushed his drink away. "I'll be seeing you, Blackwell."

Cautiously, Slocum started walking out of the Crystal Palace.

Midway down the bar, Slocum noticed a movement out of the corner of his vision. A tall, big-shouldered young man with cruel, wolfish eyes was edging his hand toward his pistol.

"Hey, mister," the kid said. He started to draw.

Slocum spun around and brought his booted foot against the gunman's hips. The man's body was propelled against the wall and down on the floor. Slocum aimed another swift kick into the gunman's ribs. The fallen gunhand screamed with pain.

Slocum's pistol was out now, sweeping across the shocked faces. Everyone had their hands out in the open.

A cuckoo clock in Blackwell's office signaled the hour.

A mule brayed out in the street.

Nobody moved.

Slocum backed out of the saloon.

He vanished through the swinging doors.

The man on the floor was sobbing.

"Get that dumbbell out of here," snapped Manny Fargo.

Three men picked up the gunman and carried him through the back door.

12

John Slocum left the Crystal Palace with anger boiling inside him. He felt Rodney Blackwell was behind the death of Shawnee Mike Samuelson. Blackwell did not carry a gun and probably was surrounded by gunmen.

The loyalty of most hired guns was questionable. Few men are willing to die for money. The size of Blackwell's gang was intimidating. Several men might die before Rodney Blackwell told what he knew.

Slocum was surprised to hear that Blackwell was the founder of Buffalo Center. Setting up a town took vision, foresight, and plenty of cash. Slocum wondered if there was more to Buffalo Center than Rodney Blackwell's gang. Was someone behind Blackwell, directing his actions?

Lost in thought for a moment, Slocum walked past the door of the livery stable. He backtracked, went inside, and found George Lewis sipping a cup of his home-brewed sarsaparilla.

Lewis grinned when he saw Slocum's tall frame in the office doorway. "I was worried about you," the liveryman said. "Doc said you were going to the Crystal Palace. I thought Blackwell's bunch might gun you down."

"One of them tried." Slocum sat down on the horsehair sofa.

"I take it he didn't succeed."

"He'll be breathing with pain for a few weeks."

Lewis laughed. "You hit him in the ribs?"

"No, I kicked him there."

"Lordy be! That must've been something to watch. Tell me about it, John Slocum, and liven up my day. I'll get you a nice cup of sarsaparilla."

"Later maybe. I'm trying to sort things out. Do you make protection payments to Blackwell?"

"Sure. Everybody who runs a business in town pays."

"How much?"

"Ten percent of what we take in."

"How do they know what you make in a week?"

"They don't," said Lewis. "Truthfully, they don't. But this is a real small town. Most folks know how much trade is done at a business. Blackwell's boys also keep a real sharp eye on things."

"How much do you pay a week?"

"I get along with the boys," Lewis said. "Or maybe they get along with me. People who have horses need a place to keep them. All those men in Rodney's gang keep their horses here. That more than pays for anything I give back."

"They ever threaten you?"

"Shucks! I get along with those boys! I wouldn't fight them. First, I wouldn't win, and folks in a town should pull together. A couple of the men in the gang are teaching my boys to shoot a rifle. Blackwell, now he's a kind of gambling, drinking, and hard-living cuss. But as long as people make their payments, he leaves them pretty much alone."

"How many hijackings has there been of hide wagons?" Slocum asked.

"That's an entirely different matter," Lewis answered. "A lot of them. Maybe two wagons a week."

"How many hides on two wagons?"

"Oh, about five hundred for a big wagon like Mike's Studebaker." Lewis rolled his eyes up and did some mental calculations. "A small wagon carries about two hundred hides."

"Have the losses been big or little wagons?"

"All kinds."

"So Blackwell's gang could be making off with seven hundred to a thousand hides a week."

"If they're doing the hijackings."

"That would be about three to four thousand dollars each week."

Lewis nodded. "I reckon so. Hides sell for about four dollars each."

"How could they be stealing so many hides without anyone noticing?"

"My gosh, John, a thousand wagons a week roll through here."

"I haven't seen that many wagons around."

Lewis explained that many of the hide wagons never came through Buffalo Center. They used back trails and direct routes to the railroad in Dodge City. He explained that businessmen in Dodge City bankrolled hunters and their crews. The investors took a share of the income earned by the crews. Many of these big outfits hired several hunters to shoot for their numerous skinning crews.

"There's a lot of those big outfits in the fields around here," Lewis explained. "The Porter boys out of Denver even use a big metal wagon that's a big oven. They cure their hides fast. They don't wait for the sun to do it."

"Do these big outfits pay Blackwell?"

Lewis looked Slocum directly in the eyes. "You better ask Blackwell about that," the liveryman said. "My gut feeling says they're not paying. More than likely, it's the little operators like Shawnee Mike who get squeezed a little bit."

"It must hurt for a man to lose a wagon full of hides."

"Sure it does," Lewis agreed. "I've noticed the hijackers don't hit the same outfit every time. They sort of move from one to another of the small hunting outfits. They don't mess much with the big operators. Lordy, Slocum, there must be five hundred crews working within twenty-five miles of this town. Buffalo hides are big business. About three million were shipped out of Dodge City last year. Now, you're sure you won't have some sarsaparilla? I can get you some in a minute."

"I'll try some later," Slocum promised. "You seen Hotchkiss around?"

"Him and that Madam Sophie are kinda sparking. Doc always sees her when he's in town. He comes back every so often to see her."

Billy Thompson, the young man on the skinning crew, was dressed for calling on Annie at Madam Sophie's whorehouse. Billy had spent thirty-two dollars at the Adams Dry Goods store on the main street in Buffalo Center. He wore his new outfit and carried his smelly work clothes wrapped in butcher paper.

Billy had purchased a new white sombrero with a genuine imitation kangaroo leather hatband. Next, Adams sold him a set of original Mexican batwing riding chaps made from black-and-white goatskins. Billy had also bought a set of ornate Mexican spurs with big chains. These were on a new pair of high-heeled, pointed-toed boots with hand toolings of a coiled diamondback rattlesnake on their sides. He also had on a red-and-white checked shirt, a green bandanna, and had doused himself liberally from a bottle of bay rum lotion.

Billy walked with a delicate step because the boots pinched his toes. The wide-brimmed sombrero kept falling over his eyes. He had spent his money with confidence that Emil Adams knew the outfitting business. Billy asked for a set of clothes worn by young gentlemen courting young girls who lived in whorehouses.

Emil Adams decided the young, blond-headed fellow was stark raving mad. No one had told the boy that you don't court women who worked in a brothel. For thirty-two dollars, Adams figured the kid could get laid for a week by a saloon lady from the Crystal Palace.

But that advice would mean the thirty-two dollars went to the local tart. So Adams cheerfully unloaded his worst buying mistakes on Billy Thompson. Adams tried to sell the young man a long white silk scarf to wear around his neck. But Billy preferred the green bandanna, and Adams decided the customer was always right.

A couple of people passed Billy on the street. They turned and stopped after Billy passed. They stared at the boy with gape-mouthed wonderment. Two drunken buffalo men saw Billy go past the window of their favorite saloon. One burly hider rubbed his eyes. His companion decided they had been on a binge long enough.

Billy Thompson was oblivious to this attention because he was in love. Even though the boots were grinding his toes into little sausages, Billy walked to the edge of town and picked a bouquet of daisies to give to Annie. Then he minced his way back to Madam Sophie's place and knocked on the door.

Madam Sophie's mouth dropped open when she opened the door. She had seen many strange men in a variety of costumes show up at the doors of her brothels. That group included the nut cases who only came out on the night of the full moon. She decided that Billy Thompson had to be ranked with the front-runners.

"Madam Sophie," Billy spoke in a stiff, formal tone. "I am here to call on Annie."

The madam suppressed her smile. She invited the young man into the parlor. Billy stubbed the pointed toes of his boots crossing the threshold. He recovered and then stumbled on the lower edge of his batwing chaps. Little bits of goat hair were shedding off onto the floor.

Madam Sophie assisted the young man to a chair.

"Annie," Billy croaked.

"She's upstairs. I'll call her." Madame Sophie went to the bottom of the stairs and yelled, "Annie! Annie! Come see your boyfriend!"

"Ma'am, I hope you won't think wrong of me for calling this way." Billy sat very erect. His back was ramrod stiff like the etchings of beaux in the magazines. Billy had read an article advising young men how to act when they called upon a girl.

"Not at all. Annie will enjoy your company. Annie is a lovely girl, but she hasn't had any experience with men."

"I . . . well . . . I'm thinking of asking for her hand in marriage."

"That would be nice," cooed Madam Sophie.

"A man needs a wife."

"I agree."

Madam Sophie turned her head when Annie came down the stairs. She made a face warning the girl not to laugh at Billy's appearance. Annie recognized the signals and came stepping blithely into the parlor.

"I brought these for you, dearest princess." Billy stood up as Annie came into the room. He thrust out his hand with the daisies, struck Annie in the stomach and, backing away, stepped on Madam Sophie's right foot.

"Damn! I think you broke my toe!" Madam Sophie hopped around the parlor, alternately limping, grabbing at her foot, and trying to remove her shoe.

"I'm sorry, Madam Sophie!" Billy started toward the woman.

"Stay away!" shrieked the madam, drawing back.

The rowel of Billy's new spur caught the end of the rolled up carpet against the wall. He pitched forward into a thudding heap on the floor.

He lay face down on the floor gasping for wind.

Hearing the commotion, the whorehouse's elderly yellow hound dog raced out of the kitchen. The animal saw Billy sprawled out on the floor. The hound grabbed a mouthful of goat-haired chaps and began to growl and shake his head furiously.

Madam Sophie looked over at this pitiful young man. He had tried to make an impression on Annie, who needed a little attention.

Madam Sophie's laughter started deep down in her ample bosom. It rolled out until she cried. Then, catching his breath, Billy Thompson was touched by the contagion of laughter. He decided laughing was better than crying. Annie joined in. The yellow hound ran around the room and barked.

Homer Hotchkiss came into the kitchen carrying three chickens he'd killed in the backyard. Hotchkiss heard the racket and peeked into the parlor. He looked at Billy, Madam Sophie, Annie, and the hound. Hotchkiss turned on his heels and retreated to the backyard.

Madam Sophie's laughter brought the girls down from their upstairs bedrooms. Soon everyone was laughing.

Between great whoops, Madam Sophie got out four words.

"Billy . . . stay . . . for . . . supper," she whooped.

Slocum ate in a small restaurant on a side street. The food was greasy, the service lousy. He wondered why he hadn't eaten some beef jerky. Sticking a toothpick in his mouth, he strolled toward the livery stable to get his horse.

Suddenly he noticed a shadow in the alley behind the Crystal Palace. The shadow was quick, furtive, and Slocum knew what was coming. The hatchet-faced drifter was about fifty feet away, a lanky man whose hand dipped down and came up with a gun. Orange flames blossomed with the roaring boom of the pistol.

Slocum felt heat as the lead whipped past his head. The

bullet chunked into a window of a shop across the street.
The hatchet-faced man was trying to disappear around the
corner of the Crystal Palace.

Slocum went into a crouch, his hand coming up with his
revolver. He hesitated because the light was dim. Then
another bullet came from the hatchet-faced man's gun. The
pistol flash pinpointed the target. The bullet barely missed
Slocum, tugging at the fabric of his shirt.

Slocum took aim and pulled the trigger. He saw the
other man driven back against the saloon wall. The
wounded man made a clawing effort with his hands and
managed to remain on his feet. Slocum fired again and the
man went down in the alley.

Slocum ran into the alley. The man was starting to crawl
away. Then he stopped and tried to bring up his gun with a
bloodied arm. Slocum kicked his wrist. The weapon went
spinning away.

Slocum pushed down the urge to send another bullet
into the man. Instead, he fanned the man for a hideout gun,
then pulled him to his feet.

The man began to make a gurgling sound. Then Slocum
noticed the blood-slick on the man's shirt. It was widening
and spreading as the man's heart pumped out his lifeblood.

Slocum heard people coming from every direction. He
didn't want one of Blackwell's gang to use him as a target,
so he stepped away from the wounded man. The hatchet-
faced man dropped to the ground with a moan.

Slocum looked down into the hatchet face. "Mister,
you've got about two minutes before you cash in. Did
Rodney Blackwell hire you?"

"Not Blackwell."

"Who then?"

"A man."

"Did he have a name?"

"He said you'd be easy to take. I was just passing
through town. I needed the money."

"What did he look like?"

A bright intensity came into the drifter's eyes. He made a strangled coughing sound. He gasped for breath that would not come.

Slocum felt the man's body go limp. He looked up. Rodney Blackwell, Manny Fargo, and the crowd from the Crystal Palace were standing a few feet away. Several members of the Blackwell gang watched the dying man with morbid curiosity.

Rodney Blackwell walked over and looked down at the dead man. "He wasn't mine, Slocum. Why would I hire a saddle tramp when Manny Fargo is on my payroll?"

Slocum couldn't answer that question.

"Anyone know this dead man?" Blackwell spoke to the crowd in the alley.

Several men moved forward for a better view.

"I saw him this morning," said Mysterious Dave Henderson. "He was in the Crystal Palace right after it opened up. He was asking about work. I told him to go out and hook up with one of the buffalo crews. The big outfits are always looking for hands."

Slocum asked, "Did he say where he was from?"

"Colorado. He just got into town this morning. Said he'd camped down by the creek last night."

"Why would he go after me?" Slocum muttered aloud.

"I can answer that, Slocum. Obviously, someone hired him," said Blackwell. "You're drawing trouble like honey draws horseflies. He wasn't working for me."

"Maybe you're barking up the wrong tree," said Manny Fargo. He had the Colt Dragoon close to his hand. "It may not be Blackwell who's after you."

"Yeah," agreed Mysterious Dave Henderson. "You check his pockets for money?"

Slocum turned out the dead man's pockets. Two gold coins slid out on the ground.

"A hungry man will do about anything for two of those," said Manny Fargo.

"But who is giving them out?" Slocum wondered.

13

After the shoot-out with the hatchet-faced man in Buffalo Center, Slocum returned to camp. He awakened the next morning to find the hiders talking excitedly. Overnight, the number of buffalo had increased out on the plains. The main part of the great southern herd was moving through to their winter grazing in Texas.

Slocum called a meeting to discuss the future of the crew. The hiders decided to continue working as a team, with Slocum as their leader. Each man would receive wages, and profits would be shared equally among the group.

After the meeting, Slocum left camp and rode out on the plains. The land was dotted with hundreds of buffalo grazing their way south. They were moving in small, scattered herds. They covered the plains like some dark, shaggy growth. Their smell was in the air—a sweaty animal odor, the aroma of fresh droppings, the scent of buffalo hair wet-

ted with morning rain. Slocum found a thicket of high
weeds that was close to one of the grazing groups of buffalo.

Dallas McGhee, the skinner, came riding up and joined
Slocum. "It always makes me feel small," said McGhee. "I
feel like God must've made this for his own private view-
ing. Men like me and you weren't supposed to see it."

Slocum felt the same way. The windswept plains had
been left alone since the beginning of time. Now the great
shaggy buffalo were being killed. An era was ending. Future generations would only hear about the great herds.

Up ahead on the vast expanse of green plains, two giant
bulls prepared to do combat. The huge animals were about
thirty feet apart, snorting and bellowing at each other. They
pawed the earth. Their sharp-hooved feet dug into the buffalo grass, throwing sod behind them.

Great heads lowered, legs pounding, they roared into
combat. Their heads smashed together with a sound like
sharp thunder. Both animals were knocked to their knees.
But they rose up and locked horns. They bellowed their
rage and anger. Their huge shoulders knotted with strength
as their flanks drove them forward.

At last, his tongue hanging out for want of breath, one
bull lost his footing. His enemy drove his horns into the
fallen bull's flanks. The wounded bull roared with pain
from the goring. He turned tail and ran away. The victor-
ious bull flexed his shoulders and strutted before the cows.

Slocum set up the tripod, rammed a fresh cartridge into
the Sharps .50-caliber, and snapped the lever shut. He
placed the gun on the tripod and lay down in the grass on
his stomach. He watched the herd for some sign of the
leader, a buffalo that acted as sentry.

"I think that old cow over on the right is the watcher,"
said Dallas McGhee. He pointed to the side of the herd.

Slocum laughed. "She's a tricky old broad!"

"Ain't she?"

The old cow was almost hidden behind two calves, an-

other cow, and two young bulls. But she was on guard—
head up, eyes moving, nostrils flared, sniffing the wind for
signs of peril. Slocum thumbed back the hammer on the
Sharps and waited for a good shot centered on the lungs.

One of the bulls wandered off. Slocum squeezed the
trigger and the Sharps boomed. The big bullet smashed
into the cow's lungs. Blood gushed from her mouth and
shot out of her nostrils. She fell over on her side.

One of the young bulls sensed danger. He walked over
and sniffed the dead cow. Slocum pushed down the trigger
guard, pulled out the empty casing, and shoved in a new
cartridge. He banged the lever shut and took aim on the
nervous bull.

The Sharps cracked, and the young bull dropped beside
the cow. Several cows and bulls walked over to inspect the
two bodies. A calf bawled beside the fallen cow. The herd,
about sixty animals, did not seem concerned.

"Dimwits!" Dallas McGhee shook his head, unbeliev-
ing. "I keep forgetting how dumb they are."

Slocum aimed in on the nervous ones. He dropped ten
animals, then poured water down the barrel of the big
Sharps. This cooled the gun barrel. He swabbed out the
water and reloaded. He killed another ten animals, then
swabbed the barrel. He shot and swabbed until the herd
was dead on the ground.

"Time for me to get to work," said Dallas McGhee. He
picked up his box of knives and his honing stone and
walked out to where the animals lay.

The crew fell into a routine. Slocum shot the buffalo and
oversaw the skinning and curing of hides. By nightfall, the
men were ready for diversion from the stench of blood and
death. Leaving one or two men as guards, Slocum led the
group into Buffalo Center for recreation.

They had a few beers or whiskies at the Hunters and
Hiders Saloon. Slocum wanted to get into Pearl Buckley's
pants. He always had good bedroom fun with lady saloon

owners and bartenders. Pearl enjoyed the attention, flirted with Slocum, and hinted that something might develop someday.

Slocum and the group always left the saloon early and stopped at Madame Sophie's bordello before returning to camp. While Slocum and the others were enjoying the ladies, Billy Thompson and Annie sat on the back porch. Sometimes they walked to the edge of town and back.

Slocum decided Billy needed help when he rode back to camp wearing the outfit purchased at Adams Dry Goods. The men provided tips to Billy on how to arouse Annie until she would welcome seduction.

Some of the hiders hinted that Spanish fly was deadly with young girls. They told stories of women who had been slipped the love potion. These women, so the stories went, had turned into insatiable nymphomaniacs. They couldn't get enough sex. They worked through a long line of exhausted Spanish-fly users, their relatives, the men of the town. Last seen, the men said, the women headed into the wilderness looking for a he-bear.

Annie was receiving tips from Madame Sophie and her whores. Make him marry you, advised the women. Get him worked up, then stop. He'll show up some evening with a preacher. The fact that a real preacher was no closer than Dodge City didn't matter, they advised.

When a man gets hard up, they said, when his tally-whacker is as hard as stone, he'll find a preacher come hell or high water. Don't give in to the sweet talk. Men will give that to young girls until you're at who-laid-the-rail.

Billy tried to be himself. He'd thrown the goat hair chaps, the sombrero, and the accessories into the bushes. There had been growling in the brush that night. Dallas McGhee said the chaps had scared off a band of lobo wolves.

Being his own man wasn't easy. Especially when Annie was so pretty, smelled so nice, and kept sneaking those sidelong glances with her blue eyes. Billy couldn't take those smoldering looks. He got all hot and bothered and his pecker took on a mind of its own.

The young man walked around with a perpetual erection. In camp, in the saloon, or on Madame Sophie's back porch, Billy's hands were always in his pockets. His manner of walking amused the crew and the whores. Head bent forward, hands in pocket, Billy kept his tail tucked behind him to hide his erection. Madam Sophie said he was sort of leaning into life, ready to spring into action any minute.

One evening Billy and Annie came outside to sit on the back porch. Annie, as usual, looked like a dream and wore a perfume given to her by one of Madam Sophie's finest producers. The whore swore the perfume would turn a monk into a crazed rapist.

Annie also looked all fresh and pretty, her long blond hair tied back with a red bow. Billy could barely sit still. He wanted to plunge his hardness into something moist, warm, and satisfying. Just pound away until Annie was reduced to a mass of quivering flesh.

The young couple heard a noise in the chicken yard out back of the whorehouse. Madam Sophie's black rooster had decided to mount a hen. He pecked the contrary pullet on the head until she held still for his quick, hard thrusts.

Annie said, "Don't get any ideas from that."

"I'm not," Billy answered.

"The man I choose must be nice and gentle."

"I'm gentle." Billy's hand felt something leap down below.

"He will respect me."

"C'mon, Annie. Let's do it now."

"No. Not until we're married."

The rooster decided to have a spectacular night. He ran over and mounted another hen, who didn't seem to mind. All Billy could see was a lot of thrusting, a bit of head bobbing, and some contented clucking.

When the rooster was done with the hen, he strutted around the hen yard for a couple of rounds. Then the old rooster remembered the treachery of the white rooster, who was starting to screw a few hens on the sly.

The smaller, white rooster was standing by the fence when the old black rooster caught him. Some real squawks came out of the chicken yard after that. The white rooster tried to get away, but the black was on him, thrusting, showing who was king of the roost.

Annie said, "That rooster ain't normal."

Billy agreed. "Does Madam Sophie know he's double-gaited?"

"She don't pay attention to the chickens." Annie picked up her bonnet. "Let's go for a walk."

"I kinda like sitting here. That rooster's worth watching."

Annie stood up. "That rooster is giving you some bad ideas."

"At least that rooster has fun."

"Lordy!" Annie stuck her tongue out at him. "There's a lot more to life than doing that."

"I wouldn't know. I never had a chance to try it." A sort of stone hardness was throbbing down below.

"I've lived with Madam Sophie, so I know what life is about," Annie reminded him. "I hear the women talk. They tell me things. Now, are you going to take me for a walk?"

Billy caught another whiff of her perfume. He wanted to rip off her clothes, tie her to a bed, and ravish her. Instead he stood up and followed the girl out into the yard. A full white moon blazed in the night sky.

Annie stopped at the back gate and looked up into Billy's face. "Are we going to get married?"

"God, yes. But I don't know how."

"I should tell you some things about me," said Annie. "My husband can't be a hider. They smell too bad."

"I'm learning to wash up."

"You couldn't tell it sometimes."

"I found out soap is tricky. It hurts your eyes."

"Well, a girl's nose is important."

Billy had never thought of that part of Annie's anatomy. "I reckon."

"My husband has got to earn a good living. I don't want hiders or cowboys."

"What else is there?" Billy wondered.

"Farming, maybe. My man would fix fences, put in crops, plow, cut wood, garden, and tend to the animals." Annie's face was beautiful in the moonlight.

"After that, I wouldn't have the strength left to make love."

"You'd find a way."

Billy let his arm brush against her breasts. Annie seemed to move forward against him.

"I don't know anything about farming," said Billy. He pressed harder against the softness of her body.

Annie pushed him away. "Don't be a brute."

"I got to have you!" cried Billy. He grabbed Annie's breast and shoved his body against her.

"Billy!" The tone of her voice was like ice water. "You love me. I'm going to be your wife."

Billy stepped back. "I want to forget farming. Get to it without all this fooling around."

"You could learn to farm."

"I ain't very smart. I'm probably a brute around women."

"You just need to relax."

"I can't relax."

"I've noticed. By the way, I want at least six or eight kids."

Billy frowned. "How many?"

"They'll be a help around the house, and they can help you with the hard work."

Billy heard Slocum call from the back porch. Time to ride back to camp. Annie raised her head for their customary good-night kiss. For the first time, her lips were parted a little bit. There was just a hint of her hot, pink tongue against Billy's lips.

All the way back to camp, Billy's tallywhacker throbbed like a demon.

A few days later, Slocum and the crew were gathering up hides when a middle-aged man in a black suit rode into camp on a gray mule. The man swung down out of the saddle with a grunt. He was plump, of medium height, and his skin was pallid. He had the mild expression of someone who watched life rather than lived it.

"I'm looking for Mike Samuelson's crew," the man said. "I'm James Findley, a clerk at the county courthouse."

"You found us," said Slocum. "Want a cup of coffee?"

"It would be a comfort."

The cook brought over a mug of thick coffee.

The man expressed his thanks, then went on, "I rode out to see about Samuelson's estate."

"Estate?" Slocum looked dumbfounded.

Dallas McGhee asked, "What's an estate?"

"His belongings," explained Findley. "Whatever he owned. You see, the laws of Kansas take over when someone dies. The deputy sheriff said Samuelson was killed by Indians. That means his estate has to be probated. Did he leave a will?"

Slocum looked around the crew. "Did Mike say anything about a will?"

Dallas McGhee shook his head negatively. "Hell, Mr. Findley, Mike wasn't the type to figure he was going to die."

"No will," said Findley. "That means it'll take longer."

"What will?" asked Slocum.

"Probating his estate."

"How is that done if Mike didn't leave a will?"

Findley explained, "The law has provisions for that. Without a will, the judge orders the property sold off and decides where the money will go."

Slocum's eyes narrowed. "Is that a fact?"

"Yes," answered Findley. "It's part of the law code of the State of Kansas."

"Where does the money usually go?" asked Dallas McGhee.

"Well, there are expenses."

"For what?" asked another hider.

"Lawyers have to be paid."

"What for?" asked McGhee.

"Representing the estate."

"But you just said there wasn't one if Mike didn't leave a will."

"His property must be disposed of." Findley looked impatient.

"How much does the lawyer get?" asked Slocum.

"A reasonable fee."

"What about the judge?" asked McGhee.

"His time is handled in court costs."

"And if there's any money left after that?" asked Slocum.

"Then it goes to the State of Kansas. The state holds the money in trust until someone comes along to claim it."

Slocum asked, "You mean like relatives or kinfolk?"

"That's correct," said Findley. "You boys are catching on real fast."

"And what about if there ain't no kinfolk?" This came from Billy Thompson.

"Then the state keeps the money." Findley was proud of teaching the crew a little bit about law. "Now, if you men will give me a list of Mr. Samuelson's assets, we can get started."

"Now, let me get this straight," McGhee went on. "We give you the assets. What happens then?"

"I take them to the county seat and we sell them off."

"Who buys them?"

"The highest bidder."

McGhee folded his arms. "Mike didn't leave anything."

Findley looked disappointed. "Nothing at all?"

"Nary a dad-blamed thing," said Billy Thompson.

"He has an account in the Buffalo Center Bank for four thousand dollars," Findley said.

Dallas McGhee lied. "He owes us about that in back wages."

"Thirty-nine hundred," said Slocum.

"I heard in town he owned some high-priced Studebaker wagons," said Findley. "Probably like those ones sitting down at the bottom of the hill."

Slocum and McGhee spoke simultaneously.

"Slocum owns them," said McGhee.

"McGhee owns them," said Slocum.

Findley's face took on a pained expression. "Do either of you have a bill of sale for the wagons?"

"What's that?" asked McGhee.

"A paper proving you own them," Findley explained.

"Slocum can get one," McGhee went on.

"I can see we're going to have trouble over this estate," Findley said. "Who represents the crew?"

"Slocum," said Billy Thompson.

"I guess I do," the man from Georgia agreed.

"The rendezvous in Buffalo Center is this weekend," Findley said. "I've got to see some other people about various matters. Could you arrange to be at the rendezvous, Mr. Slocum, with your bill of sale for the wagons?"

"I think so."

Findley stood up. "Thank you for the coffee. I'll be in touch with you, Mr. Slocum. This weekend. At the rendezvous."

"I'll be there," Slocum promised.

Members of the crew remained silent until Findley had ridden out of earshot. Then they let loose. They cursed the Kansas State Legislature, the courthouse gang, and a government that would pull off such treachery.

"They treat Mike's stuff like it was a pie," said Dallas McGhee heatedly. "He worked hard all his life. Mike would have wanted us to divvy up his stuff. Use it to work with. He didn't buy the stuff so some fat attorneys and judge at the county seat could take a big rake-off. He'd turn over in his grave if he knew the state government was getting the rest of it."

"We'll think of something," Slocum said.

"I hope so," Billy Thompson remarked. "I wouldn't feel right if Mike's stuff got sold off at auction to the highest bidder."

14

The rendezvous was getting started when Slocum and his hiders rode into Buffalo Center that weekend. The outskirts of the town were dotted with scores of Indian tepees. Two hundred Cheyenne families had been camped there for days, waiting for the start of the celebration.

Hundreds of buffalo hunters, hiders, wagon teamsters, a few wolfers, trappers, and scores of homesteaders were gathered for the annual affair. After the silence of the plains, the tumult of the rendezvous was a welcome sound.

Guns exploded harmlessly into the air. The Dodge City Cowboy Band, a group of amateur musicians, had brought their horns and fiddles for a dance. The Atchison, Topeka and Santa Fe drum and bugle corps was featured in the railroad's hospitality tent. A group of U.S. Army soldiers set up tents for their show of force to settlers, hunters, and the Indians.

The soldiers were also in Buffalo Center to prevent any-

one from attacking the Indians for the death of Shawnee
Mike Samuelson. A group of troopers had gathered around
a whiskey barrel, singing popular songs of the day. They
were enjoying their duty, raising their voices in lusty song,
swigging from their tin cups of home-brew whiskey.

The Cheyenne Indians had been given a section of the
rendezvous grounds for their activities. They whooped and
danced to the beat of a tribal drum. Hordes of Indian
women, some scantily clad in deerskins, roamed through
the crowd. Many of these Indian women were willing to
tumble with the white men for a jug of whiskey.

Off to the side of the grounds, half a hundred warriors
were clustered around a bonfire beneath a large metal
drum. They were brewing up coffee—one of the Indian's
favorite beverages. A few drunken Indians were wandering
through the crowd, smiling happily at the white men.

The entire campground outside of Buffalo Center was a
welter of confusion. People were running everywhere,
laughing, slapping each other on the back, passing liquor
jugs, singing, whooping, and roaring like demented grizzly
bears.

Huge fires of buffalo chips burned under large chunks
of wild meat roasting for the celebrants. Boisterous men
gathered around a section of land set aside for horse races.
Indian and white horses participated in the contests, which
were ultimately won by a young Cheyenne warrior on his
pony.

Slocum and the hiders wandered through the grounds
like happy children. They met old friends, tasted rotgut and
snakebite whiskey, and took part in a few of the carnival
games set up by pitchmen. It was a time to relax, enjoy
life, and give thanks for a good season of buffalo.

Behind the carnival were the gambling games, some
outside and others set up under canvas tents. The gamblers,
thimble riggers, sham artists, bunco boys, and con men
occupied this part of the grounds. They were running
everything from rigged wheels of fortune to card games

noted for stripped decks and needle-marked cards.

Doll-faced women in low-cut dresses with painted cheeks plied their trade in still more tents. These hussies tried to pull Slocum and his hiders into their tents and down on their pallets.

"Won't take long, boys, and you'll get your guns off!" a hussy said, smiling and winking suggestively. She was a tired-looking woman, who gazed at them with blank eyes.

"Maybe we ought to get Billy laid," suggested Dallas McGhee.

"Hell, somebody would tell Annie," Billy retorted. "You guys tell them whores at Madam Sophie's everything."

"Stick with Annie," Slocum advised. "Most whores want your money and little else."

After their tour through the Devil's Half Acre, as the whore's realm had been tagged, they went in search of food. A man could eat all he wanted, free of charge. Hunters had brought in tons of buffalo meat, succulent hump cuts, tongues, livers, and flank steaks.

Fires burned under thirty antelopes. Deer, bear, prairie chickens, wild turkeys, ducks, and geese were the other meats sizzling on spits. Volunteer cooks watched the meat and cut off sizzling slabs when it was ready.

Washtubs of pinto beans were simmering over other fires. And roasting ears of corn could be had for a nickel each, the butter free, at a tent set up by a promoter from Dodge City. Coffee, lemonade, corn bread, and other delicacies were offered in the food tents.

Slocum was finishing off a piece of corn bread covered with deviled buffalo tongue when Homer Hotchkiss came rushing up.

"We've been looking all over for you," Hotchkiss said. "Manny Fargo has issued a challenge. One hundred dollars. Winner take all."

Alarm bells went off in Slocum's mind. He asked, "What kind of contest?"

"Shooting, naturally," Hotchkiss replied. "Everyone wants to see what you can do, Slocum. Folks are excited by how you plugged that drifter. They want to know who's fastest drawing and shooting, you or the master of the six-gun, Manny Fargo."

"I don't make public exhibitions," Slocum said.

"Hell, go take the hundred bucks," suggested Dallas McGhee.

"Yeah, send Fargo back to Texas," piped up Billy Thompson. "We don't need those Texans up here anyway."

Several other men came up and slapped Slocum on the back and shoulders. They suggested that buffalo hunters and hiders needed to show their prowess. After all, they said, it was all in good fun.

A half hour later, the match had been set up. The hundred-dollar purse had been tacked to a post outside the rendezvous grounds. A crowd had been collected by men running through the rendezvous shouting the contest was starting. The group gathered in a U-shape formation around the designated shooting ground. Hundreds of side bets were being made in the crowd.

Manny Fargo came strolling out of the crowd. He was dressed in new clothes. He wore a new hammer-tailed coat, red velvet vest, red cravet, and black trousers. His black boots were polished to a sheen. A pair of matched Colt .45 revolvers rested in hand-tooled holsters.

Fargo looked at Slocum with a steel gaze. "You ever tried this, Slocum?"

"It isn't even my idea."

"Mine either."

"Then what are we doing out here?" Slocum wondered.

"I think Rodney Blackwell figures he'll make a lot of money when I beat you." Fargo sounded confident.

Homer Hotchkiss walked out before the crowd. "Ladies and gentlemen," he said with an oratorical flourish, "we will witness a historic display of six-gun shooting this afternoon. The gentleman in the black attire is Manny

Fargo, the prince of pistols, from the great state of Texas and—"

Hotchkiss waited until the men born in Texas stopped cheering. They yelled, roared and shot off a few guns into the air.

"—and his opponent is John Slocum, the man from Georgia, who will represent the buffalo hunters in this demonstration of accurate shooting."

A rousing bedlam roared up from the buffalo crews in the crowd.

Hotchkiss resumed his oratory when the noise subsided.

"The rules are simple, gentlemen. My assistant is Rodney Blackwell, owner of the Crystal Palace saloon. Mr. Blackwell will throw a tin can into the air. The cans have been filled with mud to provide stability."

Hotchkiss explained that each man would take turns opening fire on the can in the air. After the first man had drawn and shot, his opponent would add his fire. Once drawn on a can, the pistols could remain in the hand until the can hits the ground.

"Do you gentlemen understand the rules?" Hotchkiss asked.

"I think so," said Fargo.

"What about a bullet under the hammer?" Slocum asked.

"However you ordinarily carry your gun," Hotchkiss said. "Is that okay with you, Manny?"

"Sure."

"Slocum?"

"All right."

"Gentlemen, let the contest begin. Slocum, you go first."

Rodney Blackwell stepped forward, looking pale in the glare of the bright sunlight.

Slocum set himself, feet slightly apart. He wiped his right hand across the front of his buckskin shirt.

"Let her go, Rodney."

Blackwell tossed a bright tin can into the air.

Slocum waited for an instant as the can climbed high into the bright Kansas sky. He drew his revolver as the can reached the top of its arc. His gun boomed and the can went higher, moving with a quickening spin.

Manny Fargo's hand slapped leather. His colt boomed, and the can spun off in a tumbling trajectory.

Slocum fired again, and part of the can was knocked off by his bullet.

"Watch this!" Fargo snapped off a shot. The can plunged toward the ground in an end-over-end tumbling motion.

Slocum grinned, took a quick shot at hip level, and the can fell into the grass.

"You're even," said Hotchkiss.

Both men reloaded.

They were also scored even on the next can.

They were reloading when someone yelled, "Watch Blackwell!"

Out of the corner of his eye, Slocum saw Rodney Blackwell throw a can into the air. He thumbed off a quick shot and smiled when his bullet struck the target.

Manny Fargo's shot caught a side of the can, making it spin out of control toward the far edge of the audience.

The spectators ducked, but Slocum held up his left hand to indicate the can was out of bounds.

The next six cans were a repeat of their earlier volleys.

Neither man moved ahead.

They were evenly matched.

After a few more cans, Manny Fargo called for time out.

"We could stand here and waste ammunition all day," the Texan said. "Why don't we call this a draw?"

"Two fast-draw experts," yelled someone out of the audience. "Somebody write a book on Slocum."

Everyone laughed.

Hotchkiss and Blackwell huddled together for a few minutes.

Finally, the patent medicine man walked over to the two men. "We're trying to figure out what to do with the hundred dollars," he said.

"Split it," said Slocum.

"Yeah, we need to pay for our bullets," Fargo added.

Hotchkiss made the announcement and split the prize money. The crowd wandered off for other entertainment.

Slocum was in a fair mood that night, walking around the torch-lit rendezvous grounds with a bottle of St. Louis premium beer in his hand. The highlight of the day had been a meeting with an old friend from New Mexico. His friend was headed east to appear in a Wild West show.

They had shared some memories, drunk a few beers, and listened to the Dodge City Cowboy Band play for the crowd. Now Slocum was thinking of finding a place to lay his bedroll for the night. He'd had enough amusement and had drunk enough beer, and his eyes were getting scratchy.

He was nearing the edge of the rendezvous grounds when a form loomed up in the darkness ahead.

Slocum shifted the beer bottle to his left hand.

"You good shot, Slocum."

The man from Georgia peered into the darkness. He grinned at Black Otter, the chieftain of the Cheyenne.

"Know how to use gun." Black Otter stepped forward, laid his hands on Slocum's shoulders. "Glad you Cheyenne brother."

Slocum smelled whiskey on the chief's breath. "You seen the shooting?"

"You good," said Black Otter. "Get rifle. We go hunt for sheep in mountains."

"Yeah, that would be nice."

Black Otter looked at the white man's eyes and knew his friend was tired. "You got place to sleep?" asked the chief.

"Not yet."

"Come with me. You sleep with Cheyenne, Slocum."

It sounded like a good idea, Slocum thought. He followed the chief to where the Cheyenne had pitched their tepees. Black Otter led him to a campfire in the middle of the campground. Braves and squaws were gathered around, drinking beer and whiskey.

Slocum's face brightened when he saw the squaw, the dark-eyed woman who had knifed her way into a buffalo belly.

Black Otter saw his friend's interest in the squaw.

"She lose man," said Black Otter. "Be fine. You friend of Cheyenne."

"Would she want me?" Slocum knew some squaws would not fraternize with white men.

"She need good man. I make her go."

Slocum grinned. "Let her decide."

"Indian tell women," answered Black Otter. "Never ask."

A half hour later, after some conversation and flirting, Slocum followed White Moon into her tepee. The musky animal smell of the squaw was exciting. She was a nubile woman with strong, firm limbs and a curvaceous body.

Inside the tent, White Moon lay down on a pallet of beaver fur. Slocum removed his clothes and joined her, aroused by the sleekness of the fur. White Moon had raised the skirt of her deerskin dress, and she rolled into his arms.

John Slocum would have liked to have seen the curving firmness of her flesh. But moving his hands over her hips and bottom, feeling the warmth and firmness of her, was a sensual experience. He knew the squaw was not an innocent woman, but he was surprised by the wanton movement of her body.

Swiftly, she took his hardness in her hands and placed it between her legs. Then her thighs tightened and he was gripped with the stroking movement of her body. She moved in an in-and-out motion, grinding against his shaft, murmuring little moans of pleasure deep down in her throat.

There was a hunger to her love, a physical need that drove her to prolong the intensity of their foreplay. She kissed him with an urgent need. Her thick, dark bush rubbed over his shaft. A moist smoothness warmed his flesh.

The scent of her body heightened her natural sensuality. Slocum became more aroused, feeling lust rising in his loins like a wild animal. He became swollen with desire.

Then, like a coquettish courtesan, she moved back away from his thrusting motions. Her strong fingers closed over his throbbing flesh.

"Nice," White Moon said. "Big!"

Slocum grew and hardened under her ministrations. White Moon knew the places to touch to increase a man's arousal. He became stone hard as she stroked him to greater size.

Now, White Moon did something and her breasts came free from the deerskin dress. They were large, round, and firm. She pressed herself against Slocum's chest, moving her nipples gently against his skin. Those swollen tips were like delicate butterly wings fluttering against him.

Slocum dipped his head and took a swollen nipple in his mouth. He sucked hard. And while she stroked his projecting hardness, he moved his fingers through the thick mass between her legs.

"I hurt . . . I want . . ." she moaned.

"Baby, you're great," Slocum answered. He placed his lips on the nipple of her other breast and felt the warm smoothness of silken flesh enter his mouth. Then his tongue swept over the hardened nipple as White Moon moaned with pleasure.

"Now, Slocum," she pleaded. "Please."

White Moon rolled over on her back, opening her legs, urging him to mount her. Vixen sounds started deep down inside her throat, the growling noise of an animal in the height of heat. It seemed as if she had been swept back to some ancient time, some primeval moment when instincts were beyond taming.

Slocum pushed her back against the satiny smoothness of the beaver fur. He rose up and brought his hardness against her body. She was moist and ready, arcing herself up to meet him. Then, as she moaned with longing, he penetrated into the moist warmth of her body. She was tight, perhaps the tightest woman he had ever known.

Her strong legs encircled his body. Her round, firm bottom began to rotate against his thrusts. In, out, in, out, the heat of her flesh tightened over his hardness.

"Don't stop," moaned White Moon.

Then, with their bodies blended together into a single hungering flesh seeking release, they seemed to rise above the earth. There was a soaring sensuality that kept them moving higher, still higher, until they reached the heavens.

Together, like two panting animals, they went up into the clouds. Together they sat on the edge of a great white fleecy mass. They looked west and saw an inviting red sun, a golden warmth, and all was fair and honest in the world.

Then, holding each other in an embrace, they leapt off the cloud, into the freefall of space. A wave of satisfaction caused their bodies to release all the pain and frustration into a pleasurable climax. And then, as the fluids drained out of their bodies, they clung together like two sated children.

White Moon was not easily satisfied. They made love again after sharing the warmth of each other's arms. Then Slocum was awakened in the middle of the night. Using her delicate touch while he slept, White Moon had moved him to a hardened arousal. Afterward, entwined in each other's arms, they slept.

15

Slocum ate breakfast with the Cheyenne tribesmen, then walked toward the main area of the rendezvous grounds. He was passing through the Devil's Half Acre—the whores' domain—when a woman screamed inside a canvas tent. The shriek was high, wailing, like the death yell of a terrified woman.

Slocum rushed over and pulled back the tent flap. Although the interior of the tent was dim, Slocum saw a burly man in buckskins holding a knife on a naked woman. The man held the knife near the woman's sagging breasts. He was grinning wolfishly.

"Jest gimme the gold piece back, babe! I may've spent the night, but you wasn't all that good!" Saying this, the man swept the skinning knife at the woman's breasts.

He chortled when the woman shrank back, slipped over a camp stool, and fell to the ground. She fell in an awkward position, eyes open, her hairy bottom exposed.

Slocum's eyes had adjusted to the dimness beyond the flap. He saw that the prostitute was Maureen Polk, the friendly lady he'd met at the Long Branch Saloon in Dodge City. She appeared to be terrified of her customer, who was half drunk.

"What I mean is you kin see all th' way to China through that big hole!" The man laughed. "Now gimme m'money and I'll go!"

Slocum spoke up. "Okay, skinner, leave the lady alone."

The man whirled around, knife thrust before him. "Who's gonna make me?"

"I will, if need be."

"Slocum! God bless you!" cried Maureen Polk, scrambling away from the man.

The man hesitated. "Your name Slocum?"

"Yep. John Slocum."

"The one who did that fancy shooting yesterday?"

"You're a smart man," Slocum answered.

The skinner holstered his blade. "I was just funnin' the lady. Nothin' meant by it. Reckon if I mosey out we can fergit this?"

Slocum looked at Maureen Polk, who was wrapping a robe around her naked body. "What do you say, Maureen?"

"Just so he gets out of here," she replied.

"Vamoose!" Slocum jerked his thumb in the direction away from the tent.

The man bent down and came through the door of the tent. "No offense, Mr. Slocum." He tipped the edge of his dusty hat and almost ran away.

Maureen came outside the tent and expressed her thanks. "He was a real yahoo," she said. "Wore me out last night, then claimed he didn't get value for his money."

"What are you doing here?" Slocum inquired.

"Making money. What else?"

"I thought you were doing okay in Dodge."

"That tinhorn was caught dealing crooked," she said.

"You know, the one I was living with. He had to leave town, so I'm traveling with him. Best bust-out gambler in the business. Even better than my dear dead husband. Of course, my dearly departed was not a magician."

"I guess I don't know your fellow."

"Sure you do, Slocum. He was going by the name of Texas Tom Schacht."

"The cattleman."

Maureen snorted. "He wouldn't know a cow if she laid on him."

"You say he's a tinhorn?"

Maureen nodded affirmatively. "Tom's in a big game over at the Crystal Palace right now. Say, my memory is coming back. Didn't he take a few dollars off you one night in Dodge? Something to do with mosquitos and switching the decks?"

"My whole roll," replied Slocum.

Maureen's hand came up to her mouth. "I forgot about that. Don't shoot him! For God's sake, he's all I got."

Slocum's eyes narrowed. "I hope you like him broke, Maureen. Or dead if he misdeals the cards."

Twenty minutes later, Slocum pushed into the Crystal Palace saloon. The bar was crowded with drinkers. The tables were filled with men playing cards. From the money on the table, Slocum knew these were high-stakes games.

Slocum nodded to Manny Fargo and a couple of Blackwell's hard cases. They were standing at the end of the bar, sipping whiskey, watching the crowd. The man from Georgia saw Texas Tom Schacht sitting at a back table. Homer Hotchkiss, Rodney Blackwell, and a big, burly man in buckskins were sitting around the table.

Slocum walked over, greeted the players, and asked, "Can I join the game?"

"The game is stud poker," answered Blackwell. "Sit down, Slocum. I'll enjoy spending your money tomorrow. You got enough money to get into this game?"

"Sure." Slocum threw some money on the table. The wad of greenbacks had been given to him by Shawnee Mike Samuelson.

Blackwell's eyes glinted with greed. "That'll be fine. Now, you know Homer. This jasper in the buckskins is Brad Gill, another hunter. And the dealer is Texas Tom Schacht, a cattleman from Texas. What was that town you're from, Tom?"

"Delhart," murmured Schacht, who was eyeing Slocum with a panic-stricken expression. "Do I know you, Mr. . . ."

"Slocum, John Slocum. We played one night with Bat Masterson and a couple others. Back room of the Long Branch Saloon."

"Lordy! I gamble with so many people." Schacht pushed his hat back.

"You should remember me." Venom edged Slocum's words. "Our game got screwed up with mosquitos."

A flicker of panic registered in Schacht's eyes. "You seen my woman around?" he asked.

"We were chatting about mosquitos."

"Dang it, Slocum. Sit down!" This came from Homer Hotchkiss. "We want to play cards."

"I'm cashing in anyways, boys," said Brad Gill. "The game's too rich for my purse. Take my chair, Slocum."

Gill slid back the chair and stood up.

Slocum sat down and looked across the green felt table. "Deal me in." He gave Schacht a deadly look. "My luck is going to change today."

A glint of acceptance showed in Tom Schacht's eyes. "You never know," he spoke with meaning. "It just might do that. I suggest you bet your cards, Slocum, and back them up with that big bankroll."

Slocum figured the gambler was giving a high sign. Bet good and hard, he figured Schacht was saying, and I'll deal the cards in your favor. It would be an easy way to repay Slocum for the trimming in Dodge City.

Slocum exchanged part of his bankroll for chips. He felt good. Everything Schacht did sent a signal to Slocum: bet heavy—the cards will be coming your way. Within an hour, Slocum's pile of chips had tripled. They were all blue chips now. The smaller denominations had been cashed in and removed from the table as a nuisance. Rodney Blackwell was the heaviest loser. Homer Hotchkiss was also down. Texas Tom was slightly ahead.

Looking up, Slocum noticed that their table had become the center of attention in the Crystal Palace. The bar was lined two-deep with onlookers whispering about the high-stakes game.

"I'm getting tired," said Tom Schacht. "Let's try seven-card stud for this round."

Slocum took that to be a signal to make some big plays.

Slocum's first card down was an ace. His second down was a king of hearts. His first card up was a three.

Rodney Blackwell was high on the table with a queen. He bet twenty bucks. Everyone stayed.

Slocum was dealt a king as his next up card. That gave him a pair. Hotchkiss had a pair of jacks showing, Schacht a pair of tens. Rodney Blackwell had only a queen and a nine in sight.

Hotchkiss was high on the table. He bet fifty bucks. Schacht met the bet.

Blackwell studied his cards for a moment. "Hell, rock it up to a hundred," he said.

A stir went around the room. The play at the other tables slowed down as attention swung to the high-stakes game. The big-money hand was coming up. Slocum and Blackwell were having a showdown over the cards.

Slocum, with his king and ace in the hole and the king and three showing, pushed in his chips. "Staying for a hundred and fifty," he said.

Hotchkiss growled, cursed, and finally met the raise. Schacht also raised.

Slocum received an ace as his third up card. He now

had two pairs, kings and aces. But down rather than up. Schacht and Hotchkiss failed to improve their strength in sight, taking a deuce and nine, respectively. The jacks held by Hotchkiss were still high on the table.

Hotchkiss checked the bet to Blackwell, hoping to discover whether the saloon owner had any power.

Blackwell had a queen, nine, and ten on the board.

"A possible straight," remarked Schacht.

"Not a bad hand for seven-card," admitted Slocum.

Blackwell counted out twenty chips. "Two hundred big ones," he said.

Slocum met the bet, staying. So did Hotchkiss, although he seemed to be reluctant. Schacht tilted the bet by fifty, obviously trying to run up the pot. At least, Slocum hoped that was what was happening.

Blackwell met the raise. "Plus three hundred more," he said, counting out more blue chips.

Blackwell's hand revealed nothing on the board except the possibility of a weak straight. Either the power was in his down cards or the saloon owner was bluffing.

Slocum decided Blackwell was bluffing. He hoped Schacht had dealt just enough good cards to keep Blackwell hoping for something big.

Schacht groaned. He tossed in his cards. "No use throwing good money after bad," he announced.

"Same way I feel," said Hotchkiss, throwing in his hand.

That left Slocum and Blackwell bucking heads.

Slocum pushed in the chips to meet Blackwell's raise. "I'll have another card," he told Schacht.

Almost three thousand dollars in chips were on the table.

Absolute silence had settled over the saloon.

Schacht flipped out the fourth up card. Slocum caught a trey. He now had three pair. Kings, aces, and treys. It was a dead man's hand, the kind of draw in seven-card stud that lured a man to ruin. Weak at the moment, of course, but possibly turning into a full house. It would help cut the tension, Slocum thought, if he knew whether Schacht was rigging the play to benefit him.

Schacht dealt the remaining card down. Slocum got an ace, filling an ace full over kings.

Blackwell didn't move a muscle when he looked at his down card.

"Your bet," said Schacht.

Blackwell pushed a thousand dollars' worth of chips into the center of the table. "Just to make the game interesting," he smirked.

Schacht looked at Slocum. "Do you want to bet?" There was a tiny, almost imperceptible nod of the gambler's head.

Slocum matched the bet and raised five hundred.

A low murmur went around the room.

Blackwell met the raise with chips and greenbacks.

"I'm calling, Slocum," Blackwell announced.

Slocum turned over his hand.

Blackwell sat for a moment, looking at the chips and money on the table. Then he folded his hand and threw the cards in the discard pile.

Excited talk erupted in the room.

Blackwell's tongue darted in and out of his mouth like a bullfrog grabbling flies. The saloon owner's face flushed as Slocum drew the money and chips to his side of the table.

"I reckon a man has a right to get even," said Blackwell.

"Anytime."

"How much have you got there?"

"About ten thousand."

Blackwell licked his lips. "Big money for a few hours of playing cards."

"You want to get even?"

"Yeah. I want another shot at you."

"Fair enough," said Slocum. "Let's play for blood. I win whole hog or walk home. There's around ten thousand on the table, give or take five hundred. I got another fifteen hundred in my pocket. All that against the Crystal Palace."

"Agreed," said Blackwell.

A low murmuring sound went across the room.

Homer Hotchkiss suddenly became very agitated. His face twisted into a dark scowl. "Rodney, use some sense. Slocum is running a hot streak."

"I can feel it, Doc. Right here!" Blackwell placed his hand over his heart. "I beat him. Relax! I got my luck under control."

"You crazy idiot! You're—"

"You seem awful interested in Blackwell's money, Doc." Slocum looked at the doctor with a curious expression.

"Naw! Nothing," said Hotchkiss with a snorting sound. "I just hate to see someone lose everything."

"By the way," said Blackwell, picking up the cards and shuffling, "this is a winner-take-all. Add all those wagons and equipment that you inherited off Samuelson."

"Sure," Slocum said agreeably. "But it goes up against your so-called insurance company."

"Rodney!" Homer Hotchkiss shouted.

"Agreed," said Blackwell. "Five-card stud is the game. Ugh! These cards are greasy! Barkeep." Rodney snapped his fingers. "Bring us a new, sealed deck."

Slocum waited until the new box of cards hit the table. Then his hand snaked out and grabbed them. "I'd say this deck has been tampered with," he said, showing the box of cards to Texas Tom Schacht. "Can you see that tiny little slit right there under the sealing wax?"

"Thunderation!" Schacht gave Blackwell an ugly stare. "Sir! You were trying to bamboozle this fellow!"

"Now, I don't know anything . . ." protested Blackwell.

A whisper moved through the room.

"I'll take your word for it," said Slocum, holding up his hand, palm out. "You'll find folks say the Slocums are an easy group to be with. We don't argue much. These cards seem to be a stripper deck. Would you verify that, Mr. Schacht?"

"I saw a deck like that once down home," said Schacht, slowly running his fingers over the edges of the cards. "Yes sir, mister. Those sure seem like strippers to me."

Another whisper buzzed the room.

"Will you shuffle them, Mr. Schacht?"

Schacht looked puzzled. "Don't you want an untampered deck?"

"Sir, I doubt the Crystal Palace has a straight deck. We'll play with this one," Slocum said. "Only we ain't playing stud poker. We're asking you to give each of us a single card, winner take all."

"That all right with you?" Schacht directed the question to Rodney Blackwell. "Course, cheaters don't have a helluva lot to say about it."

Blackwell blinked, started to speak, then watched silently as Schacht shuffled the deck.

"How do you want the deal?" asked Schacht.

Slocum shrugged. "However."

"Here's your card, Slocum. A king of diamonds, folks." The crowd pushed forward to take a look.

Schacht's fingers seemed to caress the cards.

"And here's your card." He flipped a deuce of clubs in front of Rodney Blackwell.

Blackwell stared in disbelief at the low card.

"Idiot!" screamed Hotchkiss.

Blackwell swallowed hard, eyes bulging as if he'd just witnessed a nightmare.

"You lost it all, you damned crazy fool!" Hotchkiss raved.

"What's it to you, Doc?" wondered Slocum.

Hotchkiss took a deep breath. His smile was quick and fast. "I hate to see someone mess up their lives."

Slocum stood up and spoke to the crowd. "Folks, drinks are on the house, just as soon as Rodney signs the papers giving me this place. I want to be sure everything's in writing."

Slocum stood up and walked over to where a stone-faced Manny Fargo leaned against the bar. "Any complaints, Fargo?" Slocum asked.

Fargo shrugged, keeping his hands in sight. "I roll with the punches, Slocum," answered the Texan. "No complaints. I—"

Without warning, Manny Fargo's hand slammed against Slocum's shoulder. The man from Georgia went sprawling across a table, fighting to gain his balance and draw his gun.

The table went tumbling over, and Slocum got tangled up with a couple of onlookers, ending up on the floor in a squirming nest of arms, legs, and feet. Looking up, he saw Fargo's hand dart swiftly to his holstered pistol.

The draw was smooth and fluid. The revolver was out, and an orange flash blossomed out of the barrel. Out of the corner of his vision, Slocum caught a vague glimpse of Rodney Blackwell holding a derringer, trying to aim. Blackwell was knocked back by the bullet from Fargo's gun.

Blackwell regained his balance for a minute and kept trying to bring up the hideout derringer for a shot at Slocum.

People were scattering now, moving out of the way. They crowded in front of the door, desperate people trying to get away from flying lead.

Fargo's Colt roared again. A piece of Rodney Blackwell's skull was knocked off his head. He went tumbling back, dead before his body hit the floor.

Slocum looked up at the Texas gunman, who had now holstered his Colt.

"Looks like you owe me a drink," Fargo drawled.

16

Slocum stood up and dusted off his clothes. He looked around the saloon. Everyone was staring at the bloodied body of Rodney Blackwell, who lay on the floor, blood gushing from his head and belly.

"Poorest loser I ever seen," said an old, white-bearded man.

Slocum walked over and shook Manny Fargo's hand. "I owe you more than a drink," Slocum said.

Fargo shrugged. "Maybe you can return the favor someday."

Slocum asked, "How come you were watching Blackwell? I didn't think he'd go crazy."

"I know him better than you do," Fargo explained. "Blackwell was the type to go crazy when the deal went against him."

"But to try and kill me in front of these witnesses." Slocum shook his head. "He must have been insane."

161

"Or realized he'd been snookered bad."

"I don't follow you," Slocum said.

"Hell, you can fool the yahoos in here easy enough." Fargo jerked his thumb toward the crowd. "But I'm a country boy with a suspicious mind. The play was going against Blackwell all night. I started watching that fellow Schacht. He was throwing the cards your way. Blackwell and the rest didn't catch on. You and Schacht rigged the game. And then you had the gall to blame Rodney for using a stripper deck. No wonder the poor man went crazy with frustration."

"You think we set up the game?" Slocum smiled wanly.

"Hell, I know you did."

Slocum smiled. "But you'll never know for sure, right?"

"It don't matter a helluva lot," drawled Fargo. "Now, I see Schacht is gathering up the winnings. Better get over there and get your share."

"Thanks, again."

Slocum passed a number of men struggling to get Rodney Blackwell's body onto a wide board. They were talking about whether Matt Johnson, the coffin maker, had stayed in town or gone to Dodge City to visit his brother's family.

As Slocum went past, one man reached into the pockets of the corpse. He pulled out Blackwell's wallet and handed it to Slocum. "I figure you got chips to cash in," the man said.

Texas Tom Schacht stood up when Slocum reached the gambling table. "Figured the shooting might get everyone's attention," Schacht said. "I kept my eyes on the chips and money. Want me to cash in these chips with the bartender?"

"Yeah," answered Slocum. "And take out what you figure is right for your slice. You do good work."

"We did right nice," Schacht admitted. "Too bad Blackwell lost his temper. Losers do that sometimes."

"Which is why you slip them a few bucks after the trimming?"

"Knew you'd appreciate that twenty bucks I gave you back in Dodge." Schacht grinned. "Well, things turned out all right. You own a nice saloon and gambling hall and—"

"You want to manage the place for me?" Slocum asked.

"That's a thought. I have been getting tired of moving around."

"Write yourself a good ticket," Slocum said. "You can start by watching out for my money and chips."

"I'll give you an answer later today. That all right?"

Slocum nodded. "Take care of things until then. Right now, I got to see a guy from the county seat. Make sure that Blackwell getting killed doesn't ruin my chances of taking over the saloon."

Slocum left the Crystal Palace and headed for the rendez-vous grounds. As he walked down the street, a few rain-drops splashed down out of the heavens. Slocum glanced at the western sky and saw a dark mass of clouds hanging low on the horizon. Sheet lightning bolted across the sky.

The wind had increased by the time he reached the rendezvous site. A couple of Cheyenne tepees had been blown down. Men were fighting to lower the poles on canvas tents and get them stowed and packed away.

The black clouds kept coming toward the town. Slocum noticed that they seemed to have picked up speed. The clouds were so low that it looked as if a man could reach up and touch their swirling bottom layer.

The wind was blowing away the tents in the Devil's Half Acre. Horses were neighing, tugging at their tie ropes, or running across the campground. Men and women were screaming. Slocum saw Maureen Polk battling with her tent. Suddenly the wind tore the canvas from her hands and the tent went flapping in the wind.

A pallet and a cot sailed past Slocum's head. He heard Maureen Polk's cry as she lost her footing in the wind. Her hands clawed at a clump of tall buffalo grass, trying to maintain her position. Then her grip loosened and she was rolled across the ground by the wind.

Slocum tried to reach her, but the wind suddenly increased in velocity. He fought to stay erect, then dropped to his knees and crawled toward the woman. Something struck his shoulders. He looked back and saw a tin bucket bouncing away.

A bolt of lightning cracked. There was a brilliant white flash and a terrifying crackling sound. Slocum saw a wisp of smoke rise up from the grass a hundred feet away. A canvas tent started burning. Smoke from the burning cloth was whipped away by the wind.

Slocum continued to crawl toward Maureen Polk, who was rolling across the field. Her body smashed against a large oak water barrel. She had the sense to try to hug the barrel, but her arms were unable to gain a hold. Feebly she stood up and grabbed the edge of the barrel. Blood streamed down her face.

Slocum kept moving in her direction. Now a drop of rain smacked his face. It was a huge raindrop, bigger than he could imagine. It hit with the force of a slap on his cheek. Other big drops fell on the open ground.

Slocum came to within reach of the rain barrel. Maureen Polk clung to the rim of the barrel with a death grip. Her hands were bloody. Her face had been bruised by rocks and cut by twigs and flying debris. She was shaking with fear.

Slocum grabbed the edge of the water barrel. He put his arm around the quivering woman. She trembled uncontrollably.

A solid wall of water poured out of the sky. Next, the first big hailstone struck the barrel with a clunking sound. Slocum looked around for shelter. He couldn't see anything except rain and hail. The driving thunder squall was at its peak of ferocity.

Another oak barrel went banging past. Slocum saw a little girl wearing a calico dress go tumbling behind the barrel. He could see her terrified face, her open mouth. The sound of her screaming was drowned out by the roar of the wind.

Now Maureen Polk began to scream like a crazed woman. She struggled to free herself from Slocum's arm, which encircled her waist. Her hands clawed at his face as another lightning bolt smashed around them. '

"Be quiet!" he yelled.

She continued her struggle as the thunder pounded above them. One terrifying reverberation had no time to end before another smashed down upon it. Slocum looked around and the ground was covered maybe two inches high by hailstones.

And then it was gone.

The roaring storm of wind, hail, and rain moved past. It stopped as quickly as if someone had waved his hand for silence. Even as Slocum exchanged a glance with Maureen Polk, the sun began to shine through the clouds.

"The storm is over," Slocum said, incredulously.

Maureen Polk cried.

Slocum wiped away the blood from her face. She had a series of minor cuts, but nothing of any consequence.

"You'll be fine," Slocum said.

"My tent," she sobbed. "All my clothes. What am I going to do?"

"We'll manage," Slocum said in a comforting voice. "The main thing is that you're alive."

A filtered brightness, like a cleansing illumination, came through a break in the clouds. Off to the east, Slocum could see the great mass of roiling black clouds pass rapidly away. He saw that the rendezvous grounds were soaked, that men and women were beginning to move about. The Indians were looking around for some sign of their tepees.

Everyone was happy with relief, pleased they had survived the storm. Moments before, they had been cowering from one of the great forces of nature. They congratulated each other, happy to be alive.

Slocum used his clean handkerchief to wipe the blood from Maureen Polk's face.

"Were you scared?" she asked Slocum.

"Darn right. Nature can be scary."

"You ever been in a storm like that before?"

"A couple."

"That bad?" she asked.

"One was a lot worse. But I wasn't on these flat plains."

"Am I going to be scarred?"

He shook his head, smiling. "You're going to be fine, Maureen. Maybe ten days to let the abrasions heal up. Nothing serious. You're going to be as pretty as ever."

"Thank God! There ain't much call for whores with a scarred face."

"Now we'd better get into town," Slocum said, pretending not to be worried. Both times he'd been in a thunder squall, the first storm had been followed by one that was even worse. A sense of dread deadened his spirits as he glanced toward the west. But there was nothing but sunshine out there.

They started walking back to town. Slocum looked around at the people who were walking along beside them. There were at least a hundred of them, most of the women and children with cut or bleeding faces. They hurried toward shelter, some house or business place to clean up and become human again.

Slocum cast a look to the west. A sickening apprehension twisted in his stomach. It seemed impossible that so large, so vast a cloud could form so rapidly, but it was out there now, a few miles away, a mountain of roiling dark clouds with flashes of lightning glittering like jewels in the midst.

"Let's hurry," Slocum said. He pulled Maureen along.

A man with a bad cut on his jaw hastened along beside

Slocum. "You seen it?" The man jerked his head to the west. "We better get inside."

"Keep going," Slocum encouraged Maureen. "We got about another block to go."

Slocum glanced over his shoulder. The cloud mountain had grown darker, a mass that twisted and roiled with quick variations. The gigantic cloud was now high enough to blot out the sun. It was dark, and stupendous in range. It extended over the entire western part of the sky. It started to tower above itself, reaching out in a frightening overhang that seemed ready to topple any instant.

Under this great overhang were scores of smaller clouds, dark and menacing thunderheads, white clouds that looked like steam roiling up from Hades. These smaller clouds were moving low above the plains, so low a person might reach up and touch them.

Slocum kept looking back. He stepped crookedly, lost his footing, and fell into a puddle. The water had been chilled by hailstones; he got up feeling numb and cold.

"Ohmigawd!" Maureen Polk looked west with a wide, intense stare. She pointed a wavering finger at the great storm coming toward them.

Slocum brushed off the mud and mire on his clothes. He stood looking to the west. The dark mass of clouds, large and small, now towered from the ground to the heavens. The horizon was covered with the storm clouds, which looked throughout to be in a chaotic, twisting motion.

Some of the smaller clouds beneath the underhang shot up into the air as if propelled by an explosive force. Other clouds seemed to be sucked down by an equally violent power. Some clouds rushed to the right, others to the left, upward, downward, under the gigantic mother cloud. They seemed drawn and repelled by some irresistible power.

The whole view was so powerful that Slocum wondered if this was the way the world would end. These smaller clouds were nothing compared to the bone-chilling appearance of the mother cloud. It was a solid mass of blackness from the plains into the upper heights of the heavens. And it was moving toward Buffalo Center with a promise of terror and destruction. And before it, like some lantern from Hades, the cloud threw a dark greenish light that cast a spectral glow over the plains.

Maureen Polk was awestruck by the immensity of the storm. "My God! That thing is awful. What are we going to do?"

Slocum's face was white, strained.

"Look at that!" Someone screamed.

The spinning force was obscure at first, only a tiny thing not much thicker than a dust devil. Then it grew with unimaginable speed.

It became gigantic, powerful, and dangerous.

It rushed over the plains with the speed of a runaway locomotive.

It pushed through the smaller clouds and came out into terribly clarity.

It was a Great Plains tornado.

Maureen Polk had never seen a tornado. She thought of it as a tower of ivory, except this malignant force was spinning, twisting with snakish movement. The sound of it came to them like the bellow of a million bull buffalos roaring their anger, wrath, and pain. It moved across the prairie toward the town at a rapid pace.

The dreadful pillar stood at least a mile high.

"Get down!" cried Slocum above the oncoming roar.

He grabbed Maureen's arm and pulled her into a ditch. He pushed her tightly down, keeping his arm on the back of her head. There were some things, he decided, best not seen. And the storm was one of those things. The advancing tornado was of the proportions that boggled the human mind.

Darkness spread over the land. The titanic sound was like a million freight engines hurtling out of control.

The screaming fury of the storm was upon them.

The tornado was like a living creature propelled by an unlimited power lusting for the destruction of everyone.

The crashing of trees, rocks, and creatures in the twisting tornado was unbelievable.

The earth shook as if beset by a gigantic earthquake.

Tons of masonry were ripped out of a building and sucked up into the maelstrom.

Buildings were instantly whipped away into oblivion.

Slocum kept his head down, but a sidelong glance showed a wagon and horse moving through the air.

He heard the faint cry of a human, then saw an antelope being propelled through the tornado, end over end.

Something struck the ground beside his head. He looked and saw a brick with a single straw driven through the middle.

Then a half-dozen fish flew past.

And then the great tornado was gone.

The roar receded to the northwest of Buffalo Center.

"Oh! We're alive," said Maureen Polk. "Bless God, we're alive!"

The roar of the storm receded as Slocum stood up. He helped Maureen to her feet.

They looked about them, still dazed.

Several houses on the side streets had been destroyed. These structures had been smashed into twisted rubble. Trees were uprooted. People lay about on the ground, moaning, crying. Some appeared to be badly hurt.

Slocum looked toward the main street.

The livery stable and all of the horses were gone.

A horse's collar had been driven through a tree.

The ruin was terrible and widespread.

Slocum turned and saw that Maureen Polk was crying.

Her gaze was on a young man who lay limply like a dishrag in the ditch behind them. He was dead.

17

Dazed, his ears ringing from the roar of the tornado, Slocum looked around. Most of the stores beyond the livery stable were destroyed. Several structures had just vanished. Half of the gunshop had been destroyed; the remainder of the shop was untouched. Revolvers and rifles remained on their wall pegs. A stack of papers was stacked neatly on a countertop.

Taking hold of Maureen Polk's arm, Slocum walked toward the center of town. The stone structure of the bank building was twisted and smashed. A couple of saloons were smashed in, their timbers and roofs strewn about.

Amid all the destruction, sitting as if a storm had never happened, was the Crystal Palace saloon. People were starting to come out of the building, blinking at the destruction, seemingly unable to believe their eyes.

Texas Tom Schacht ran toward Slocum and Maureen. "You all right?" he asked.

"We're fine," Slocum answered.

"Baby, I was scared for you." Schacht ignored the blood on Maureen's face and took her in his arms.

Slocum walked to where a crowd was gathered in front of the saloon. He saw Homer Hotchkiss standing by the batwing doors with a stunned expression on his face.

"Doc, we got to get organized," Slocum said. "We can turn the saloon into a temporary hospital. Where's your medical bag? You're going to be needed."

"I didn't bring it with me," Hotchkiss said.

"Well, maybe we can rig something up." Slocum turned around to where several hunters, hiders, and gunmen were standing. "We're going to need people to search the houses and find anyone who's hurt."

Dallas McGhee came running up. "We need help down at the Hunters and Hiders," he shouted. "Two guys are trapped under a wall."

Several men went running off, led by the skinner.

Manny Fargo came out of the Crystal Palace. "Lord, what a mess," he said. "This is the worse thing I've ever seen. Anybody killed?"

Slocum gave a friendly slap to Fargo's shoulder. "We're going to need someone to check out the other side of the street," he said. "Take some of these guys. Make sure nobody is buried under any rubble."

Fargo looked over at several members of the former Blackwell gang. "You guys get the lead out," he said. "Make yourselves useful and come along with me."

Fargo led the group across the street. One gunman was wondering how an entire livery stable and all the horses could vanish.

"You heard the tornado's noise," Slocum heard Fargo say. "They got a lot of power."

"But a dang livery stable? That's unreal," answered the gunman.

"Kinda makes you think about getting religion, don't it?" Fargo remarked.

The group was too far away for Slocum to hear the young gunman's reply.

"Come with me," Slocum told some buffalo men. "We'd better check this side of the street." Slocum started off, then turned back and spoke to Homer Hotchkiss. "Doc, get moving. Set up someplace for an operating table. We're bound to have injured people."

Already, people were straggling in from the direction of the rendezvous area. One big, burly hunter in buckskins walked with a limp, supported between two friends. He had an ugly wound on his head.

"Doc will take care of you." Slocum pointed the bleeding man toward Hotchkiss.

"Thank God we got a doctor in town," said the hunter, standing between his two friends. "I'm in good shape compared to some folks that are coming in."

Slocum and his men went off to check the ruins of the business buildings. They found an old man trapped under the debris of Matt Johnson's shop. Several minutes were required to remove the timbers and rescue the elderly man.

They went along the street and found several business buildings in various degree of ruin, but they didn't find anyone else trapped in the wreckage.

A man staggered up with a profusely bleeding face.

"Jesus! Get down to the Crystal Palace," Slocum said. "We're turning that into a hospital."

"I ain't too bad," protested the man. "I just need something to wipe away the blood."

"What happened?" Slocum looked around and saw a man's shirt lying in some timbers. "Here, wipe up with this."

"Chrissakes, just my luck. I was standing by a big window when the thing went through," announced the man, wiping his face. "Dang glass exploded and went all over the place. Here, that'll do me. Somebody said the whorehouse got hit bad."

Slocum and his group hurried over to Madam Sophie's

place. The house had been smashed by the tornado. The walls had been knocked inward; the roof and second story had collapsed into the basement.

Lil came running up when Slocum and his men came into view. "Hurry! Hurry!" she yelled. "We think Sophie and Annie are trapped in the basement."

Lil explained that Sophie must have seen the oncoming tornado through a window. She had called a warning upstairs to her whores. Annie was downstairs with Sophie, peeling potatoes in the kitchen.

"We think they went down into the basement and are trapped down there," said Lil. "We've started pulling back the timbers. We need more help and someone who knows how to do it. We're afraid everything is going to fall in on them."

"Let's take a look," Slocum said.

The men started to work, kicking away the rubble, pulling away as much smashed timber as they could. Slocum wondered if anyone could remain alive down below in that wreckage. Other men arrived and, taking an example from Slocum, began to pull away the debris.

"Listen! I hear something!" Slocum motioned for the others to stop working.

They stood and listened. From down below came a faint voice.

"Someone's alive!" cried Lil.

"Let's get this stuff out of the way," Slocum said.

Some men pulled away more timber. Other men tossed stones and pieces of furniture off to the side. Still others lifted timbers out of the way, or rearranged large beams to open a way into the basement.

Billy Thompson came running up, his young face flushed from inner turmoil. "How's Annie?"

Lil told him she was trapped in the wreckage.

"We've got to save her!" Thompson leaped into the rubble and began throwing out debris in a frenzied manner.

"Get away!" Slocum shouted. "You're going to knock everything in on them."

One of the men and Lil grabbed the young man's arms.

"Come on, son," the man said. "You're too worked up. We'll get them out."

"Sit over here for a minute with me," said Lil.

"Keep him out of the way," yelled one of the men, throwing aside more timbers.

Again, and with tremendous frustration, Slocum and his men tore into the ruins. Part of the basement walls could be seen underneath a couple of twisted timbers. Working carefully, they pried away these big beams and used two-by-fours to lever up part of the kitchen wall.

On his hands and knees, Slocum crouched at the entrance of a small opening into the basement.

"Anyone down in there?" he shouted.

"Do you hear Annie?" Billy Thompson asked Slocum as he stood near the opening.

Slocum yelled down into the little opening again.

No answer was forthcoming.

"I'm going in there," said Slocum.

"It looks too full of stuff," said one of the men. "The whole thing may cave in on you."

"I'll go in with a torch," said Billy Thompson.

"No," Slocum said. "It might catch fire."

"We ain't even sure anybody's down there," added one of the workers.

"We heard that noise a few minutes ago," pointed out another man.

"Hell, that could have been a cat," remarked another worker.

Just then, a thin, reedy wail came up out of the darkness.

They kicked and pulled at the debris until the opening was a bit larger. The wreckage refused to move.

"Get Moose over here," someone said. He stopped and

yelled at a tall, muscular man who seemed to deserve the nickname.

"What're you trying to do?" asked Moose, running up.

"Enlarge this opening," said Slocum. "I want to go in."

Moose studied Slocum for a minute. "Somebody's down there?"

"We think so."

"Stand back," Moose said. He balanced himself on a thick beam of wood, then stepped back and studied the wreckage for lay and angles. "I want to be sure where to kick it."

"Hurry! We don't have much time!" This came from Billy Thompson. "Annie needs help."

Moose took another thirty seconds to study the wreckage. Then he moved to the left, balanced himself on the beam, and raised his booted foot.

"This is the best I can do," he said.

The massive foot smashed against a piece of wreckage. Nothing happened.

"Damnation!" Moose swore like a drunken sailor. "That stuff is stuck tight in there."

"Billy!" yelled Slocum. "Get me a torch started. Quick! Nothing big."

"Anybody got a lucifer?" yelled the boy, running around pulling strips of wallpaper off the fallen walls. He wadded up these strips as Lil came up with a lucifer match.

Billy got the paper blazing, and Lil added some dried grass to the flames. Another of the whores added some tiny slivers of wood to the fire. Then they set several small pieces of lumber in the flames to burn.

Meanwhile, Moose stood on the beam and stared at the debris. "Everything has a fulcrum point," he declared. "I just got to get this mess figured out."

Moose bent down, cocked his head, and viewed the rubble from another angle. "That's it over there," he said pointing to a square piece of lumber. "If I kick that away the whole thing will open up. Either that or it'll fall into the basement."

"You don't know which?" demanded Slocum.

"Hell, this stuff's too crazy," Moose snapped. "Too many pieces are all switched around in there. You want to risk it?"

"We got no choice," Slocum said. "Kick the hell out of it."

"You got it," Moose said.

He stood up on the beam, raised his booted foot, and took careful aim at the square piece of wood. His foot came out, slamming against the block.

The wreckage gave a sickening lurch, groaning and squeaking.

Moose screamed with pain. He had torn the side of his trousers and gashed his leg on a hidden nail.

"You hurt?" someone asked.

"No, I'm squalling because I'm half wildcat," snapped Moose. "Of course I'm hurt, you dumb ass."

The wreckage looked hopelessly jammed together.

"One more time," Slocum suggested.

"Well, hell, I've ruined my leg anyway."

Moose kicked at the square block again. Nothing happened.

"Another try?" someone pleaded.

"If I don't bleed to death." Blood was flowing freely down the big man's leg. "Here goes!" Moose kicked the block with all of his strength.

The timbers hesitated for a second, then made a creaking movement. The opening widened up.

"Get him a torch," Moose said, limping out of the wreckage onto firm ground.

Slocum was already thrusting his legs into the hole. His lower body went in easily, but he had to squirm and wiggle to get his shoulders through the space. Two men pushed from the top, literally shoving Slocum down into the basement. He gashed his arm on a nail, or something sharp, going down.

He looked up when his feet landed on the basement floor.

Moose was standing by the hole with a torch.

"Be careful," admonished the big man. "We don't want a fire."

"I got it," Slocum said. He took the torch, held it low, and glanced around.

Debris was scattered all about the basement. A large beam was slanted off to the right at a forty-five degree angle. Off to the left was a small opening in a massive pile of debris. The path ahead was blocked.

Slocum moved to the left, exploring the thin passage through the debris. He moved a couple of pieces of lumber out of his path. That opened up a portion of the basement.

Slocum held the torch above his head. He was already past a point when he heard a thin, reedy moan behind him. He stepped back and the torchlight brightened the area. A long blond strand of hair was peeking out from under a large section of wallboards.

"I found someone!" Slocum yelled to the men above.

Several minutes were required to get Annie's body from under the debris. Then Slocum picked up the girl and carried her to the opening. Pushing from below, while Moose and Billy Thompson pulled up, Annie was rescued from the dark and dangerous basement.

"Gimme your hand," Moose yelled down to Slocum after the girl was out. "I'll pull you up."

"I'm going to look for Sophie," Slocum answered. "Send another torch down."

With the new torch, Slocum moved deeper into the basement. "Hello!" he called. "Anybody down here?"

A faint whisper came through the darkness.

"That you, Sophie?"

"Over here," came a hoarse whisper.

Using the thin light of the torch to guide him, Slocum

worked his way through the debris. The timbers and broken wood were a tangled mess. His passage through the basement was slow. Before he moved a piece of wood out of his way, he had to test to see if the entire mess would come tumbling down.

Testing the wood, pulling and pushing it out of his path, broke Slocum's fingernails. His hands were cut and bleeding. Still he continued through the dank darkness. He was tugging at a fallen crossbeam when a voice came out of the darkness.

"Don't mess with that one," said Madam Sophie in a faint whisper. "That's holding the big cooking stove up."

"I'll get you out in a minute," Slocum said. "Are you okay?"

"I ain't going noplace," said Sophie. "My legs and lower body are crushed. I've been out for a spell. Just come to my senses a minute ago."

Slocum found the madam trapped under a massive tangle of wood and stone.

"I think the basement wall and part of the house got me." Sophie smiled as Slocum came into view. "Oh, that's you. Might know it would be a dang fool like you coming in here, Slocum."

"Always trying to please," he grinned.

"Annie's down here someplace."

"I found her. Are you in pain?"

"Not more than I can handle until I cash out," Sophie replied. "Now, I want you to promise me something. And just remember that a deathbed promise can't be broken. Will you give your word?"

"Yes, ma'am."

"I want you to be sure Annie gets a chance at life."

"You want her and Billy to get hitched?"

"Just keep her away from that philandering husband of mine," Sophie said bitterly. "I've been noticing him lately. He keeps watching her. Seems like his eyes are undressing her."

"Your husband?"

She smiled. The feeble torchlight flickered over her bruised face. "I was just a young girl fresh off the farm in Missouri. He promised me the world with a ribbon on it. What I got was a cathouse to run when we hit the next town. My whole life has been spent in a cathouse. I run the girls while he pulled off his robberies, murders, and other crimes."

"Who is your husband, ma'am."

"I think you know. Leastways, you were smart enough to figure it out." Sophie's voice was weak, thinner. "Don't you, Slocum?"

"I think so."

"He ran the whole shebang around here," Sophie went on. "Rodney Blackwell was just a front man. Blackwell couldn't think up the schemes like my husband. But Rodney was good carrying out orders. Rodney squeezed the hunters and hijacked the hide wagons with that gang of toughs. But Rodney never killed except for that one time when he had to leave home. He—"

Sophie started to cough. Blood came drooling out of her mouth.

"You better take it easy," Slocum said.

"I'm not going anywhere," the woman replied. Her voice was low, edged with pain. "I got to finish. My husband killed that friend of yours, Shawnee Mike. Come back here after selling the hides in Dodge City. He had a big wad of money. Lord, he made it by the bale! But he spent all of it on those fancy women in Kansas City, St. Louis, and Chicago. Slocum, I'm going to die any minute. I want to know that you'll stop Homer from killing anymore."

"I will," Slocum promised.

"He never was a doctor."

"I figured that out this afternoon."

"All he ever did was kill people." Her hand came up and gripped his wrist. "Stop him! He's bad news!"

She closed her eyes. Her face tightened up as if she was seeking a last vestige of strength. "Pray with me," she pleaded.

Slocum began, "The Lord is my shepherd, I shall not want. . . ."

She repeated the words of the prayer after Slocum, whispering in a weak voice.

"And, lo, though I walk through the valley of the shadow of death, I shall fear no evil . . ."

Slocum peered into the woman's face.

Madam Sophie was dead.

18

Slocum crawled up out of the basement. He explained to everyone that Madam Sophie was dead. He drank a dipper of water and saw that Billy Thompson and Lil had brought Annie back to consciousness. Thompson said the girl didn't seem to be hurt, except for the shock of her ordeal.

While the other men began to remove the wreckage to get to Sophie's body, Slocum brushed himself off and adjusted his clothing and gunbelt. He walked toward the Crystal Palace saloon—the last place he'd seen Homer Hotchkiss.

The saloon was a makeshift hospital. Injured people were lying on the floor. They were being tended by volunteers. Texas Tom Schacht and Manny Fargo were directing the operation. Slocum made a quick count and decided that around sixty people were receiving attention. He didn't see Hotchkiss in the crowd.

Slocum walked over to where Manny Fargo was tearing

a bedsheet into bandage strips. "You seen Hotchkiss?" he asked.

"That two-bit shyster." Fargo ripped another strip off the sheet. "He claimed to be a doctor, then almost fainted when we brought in the first person with a real bad injury."

"Where's he now?"

"He went out back. I guess he needed the fresh air." Fargo yelled at a young gunman to come and get the bandages.

"How're things going?" asked Slocum.

"We're managing. Just barely," replied the gunfighter. "I've sent a rider into Dodge City to bring out some medical help. They should be here tomorrow at the earliest. We have about twenty dead. Another hundred with injuries."

"I'll be back in half an hour." Slocum started to walk away.

"We can use you now," snapped Fargo.

"I got a showdown with Hotchkiss," Slocum said over his shoulder.

Fargo called, "He and Blackwell were pretty thick."

Slocum walked out the back door of the Crystal Palace, stood in the alley, and looked in both directions. There was no sign of anyone, except for an Indian brave who was hobbling toward the saloon.

Slocum asked, "How did your people do?"

He saw the blankness in the Indian's face, then used sign language. The brave signed back that two Indians had been killed, both braves. A half-dozen Indians had serious injuries.

Slocum signed that the Indian should have the injured come to the saloon for treatment. The Cheyenne started hobbling back to Black Otter's campsite.

Slocum walked down the alley. He wondered where Hotchkiss was hiding out, assuming the man was still in town. He couldn't know that Sophie had made a confession before her death, but he might have fled after people discovered his lack of medical knowledge.

Slocum came out of the alley and saw Homer Hotchkiss walking down the street. "Hey, Doc!" he shouted. "Wait up."

Hotchkiss stood in the street until Slocum came up. "You did a magnificent thing," Hotchkiss said. "Risking your life to save Annie. She's a splendid young lady, and I've decided to pay for her future schooling. The girl will need someone to look after her, now that Madam Sophie is gone."

"And you've got enough money to do it?"

"Certainly," Hotchkiss said. "I live a frugal life. The bank account isn't much, but if I live sparingly . . . well, I believe in helping someone in need."

"Like Shawnee Mike Samuelson?"

Hotchkiss gave Slocum a sharp look. "What's that supposed to mean?"

"Sophie wasn't dead when I got to her."

"Oh." Hotchkiss tried to look unconcerned, but his eyes betrayed his nervousness.

"She talked." Slocum watched the white-haired murderer.

"That would be like the old bitch," Hotchkiss snarled. His hand edged into the pocket of his coat. Slocum saw the bulging outline of a hideout pistol.

Slocum drew and fired at point-blank range.

Hotchkiss stepped back, a crimson blotch on the front of his shirt. "You killed me," Hotchkiss gasped.

He wavered for a moment, stumbling back a step. Then Homer Hotchkiss fell into the street on his back.

Slocum turned away, holstered his gun, and walked toward the Crystal Palace. His help would be needed tending to the injured. After that, he would see that Billy Thompson and Annie received title to the saloon. Maybe Texas Tom Schacht and Manny Fargo would stay on to help them. He had other loose ends to tie up, like settling Shawnee Mike's estate.

What the hell, Slocum figured. He could be on a trail out of town within a week.

JAKE LOGAN

___ 0-425-09088-4	THE BLACKMAIL EXPRESS	$2.50
___ 0-425-09111-2	SLOCUM AND THE SILVER RANCH FIGHT	$2.50
___ 0-425-09299-2	SLOCUM AND THE LONG WAGON TRAIN	$2.50
___ 0-425-09567-3	SLOCUM AND THE ARIZONA COWBOYS	$2.75
___ 0-425-09647-5	SIXGUN CEMETERY	$2.75
___ 0-425-09783-8	SLOCUM AND THE WILD STALLION CHASE	$2.75
___ 0-425-10116-9	SLOCUM AND THE LAREDO SHOWDOWN	$2.75
___ 0-425-10419-2	SLOCUM AND THE CHEROKEE MANHUNT	$2.75
___ 0-425-10347-1	SIXGUNS AT SILVERADO	$2.75
___ 0-425-10555-5	SLOCUM AND THE BLOOD RAGE	$2.75
___ 0-425-10635-7	SLOCUM AND THE CRACKER CREEK KILLERS	$2.75
___ 0-425-10701-9	SLOCUM AND THE RED RIVER RENEGADES	$2.75
___ 0-425-10758-2	SLOCUM AND THE GUNFIGHTER'S GREED	$2.75
___ 0-425-10850-3	SIXGUN LAW	$2.75
___ 0-425-10889-9	SLOCUM AND THE ARIZONA KIDNAPPERS	$2.95
___ 0-425-10935-6	SLOCUM AND THE HANGING TREE	$2.95
___ 0-425-10984-4	SLOCUM AND THE ABILENE SWINDLE	$2.95
___ 0-425-11233-0	BLOOD AT THE CROSSING	$2.95
___ 0-425-11056-7	SLOCUM AND THE BUFFALO HUNTERS	$2.95
___ 0-425-11194-6	SLOCUM AND THE PREACHER'S DAUGHTER (On sale November '88)	$2.95
___ 0-425-11265-9	SLOCUM AND THE GUNFIGHTER'S RETURN (On sale December '88)	$2.95
___ 0-425-11314-0	THE RAWHIDE BREED (On sale January '89)	$2.95

Please send the titles I've checked above. Mail orders to:

BERKLEY PUBLISHING GROUP
390 Murray Hill Pkwy., Dept. B
East Rutherford, NJ 07073

NAME_____

ADDRESS_____

CITY_____

STATE_____ZIP_____

Please allow 6 weeks for delivery.
Prices are subject to change without notice.

POSTAGE & HANDLING:
$1.00 for one book, $.25 for each additional. Do not exceed $3.50.

BOOK TOTAL	$_____
SHIPPING & HANDLING	$_____
APPLICABLE SALES TAX (CA, NJ, NY, PA)	$_____
TOTAL AMOUNT DUE PAYABLE IN US FUNDS. (No cash orders accepted.)	$_____